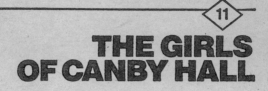

11

THE GIRLS OF CANBY HALL

WITH FRIENDS LIKE THAT

EMILY CHASE

D0039386

SCHOLASTIC INC.
New York Toronto London Auckland Sydney Tokyo

ISBN 0-590-33401-8

12 11 10 9 8 7 6 5 4 3 2 1   3   5 6 7 8 9/8 0/9

Printed in the U. S. A.   06

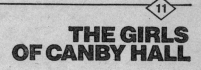

THE GIRLS OF CANBY HALL

11

WITH FRIENDS LIKE THAT

THE GIRLS
OF CANBY HALL

CHAPTER ONE

Faith Thompson shouldered her way into Baker House, puffing and struggling with the wonderful little antique table that Mr. and Mrs. Druyan had just given her. The couple who served as houseparents in Addison House were "going modern," they said, and everything old was up for grabs. Faith had decided that she and her two roommates, Dana Morrison and Shelley Hyde, *needed* this table. Room 407, the place they called home, would be positively transformed by its addition.

As Faith staggered into the front hallway, she caught a glimpse of Alison Cavanaugh, their housemother, counting a stack of fliers. "Oh, good!" she exclaimed, sweeping a lock of her reddish-brown shoulder-length hair off her forehead as she spotted Faith, "I've been looking for someone to pass these out. Faith, would you be a sweatheart and —?"

Faith's dark brown skin shone with the

exertion of her labors. She put the table down, pausing to wipe off the sweat that was creeping down from beneath the band she wore on her short afro. Then she shrugged off her parka and placed it on the table top. "Spare me the sweethearts, Alison. Just tell me to do it. I feel like a pack horse today, anyhow."

"Nice table." Alison eyed it appraisingly. At twenty-six, Alison was the youngest of the houseparents at Canby Hall. She was close to the girls not only in age, but also in taste. They rarely disagreed on much of anything.

"Isn't it great? It was a gift to Room 407. Now all I have to do is get it up there." She shrugged and stuck the fliers on top of her parka. "A couple extra pounds won't matter, I guess. What's the flier say?" she asked on her way up the curving, oak staircase.

"Ms. Allardyce has invited us all to a special surprise assembly tomorrow. Isn't that sweet of her?" Alison made a face. Patrice Allardyce, the austere headmistress of Canby Hall, was known for her lack of sympathy toward those who didn't toe the mark — consequently, faculty as well as students avoided saying anything overtly nasty about her. That didn't mean they had to sing her praises, though.

"Oh, boy," Faith grunted as she reached the first landing. "We get to rise and shine an extra half hour early tomorrow."

"Forty-five minutes!" Alison corrected her cheerily.

Faith grumbled under her breath and kept climbing. If she stopped, she was sunk. It took her exactly ten minutes to get to the fourth floor landing, and when she took the last step, she set the table down with a resounding thud.

"Oh, look, Dana! It's gorgeous!" Shelley Hyde, her blonde curls bobbing, came racing down the corridor toward Faith. Dana, a tall, leggy brunette, was barefoot and her hair was still wet from her shower, but she followed right behind her roommate.

"I'm glad you two like it," Faith said with a grin, patting tht marble fondly. "Because I wasn't about to lug it back if you didn't. Give me a hand or three, would you?"

Together, the girls lifted the table and trudged into their room. Typically, things were strewn around everywhere, except in Shelley's corner where they were meticulously in place.

"Where does this go?" Shelley mused, absently picking up one of the fliers that lay on the table top.

"Let's shove Faith's desk over near the window and put the table between my bed and Shelley's," Dana suggested, her mind's eye arranging everything in a new design. Her ambition was to be an architect someday, and she loved sculpting space. With her

keen eye, and the impeccable taste her
mother, a buyer for a classy New York department store, had helped her develop, Dana always seemed to know what went with what,
and where.

"Why is there *another* assembly?" Shelley
complained, throwing the flier down on her
bed and diving right after it. The girls had
moved their bedframes to the storage room
when they'd first come to Canby Hall a year
ago, since they liked the look of mattresses on
the floor covered with quilts and pillows. It
just took a little longer to get up in the morning because they had farther to rise.

"There is always another assembly, my
friend," Dana said philosophically, helping
Faith put the table in place. "That is the rule
of the jungle. When Ms. Allardyce calls, we
listen." She beat her breast, giving a Tarzan
whoop. "Don't you know that by now?"

"Back home in Iowa," Shelley grimaced,
"we used to call assemblies 'arch-enemies'!
Guess why."

"Hey, that's pretty good. Wouldn't think a
buncha hicks could think up something that
smart," Faith chuckled.

"Thanks a lot, Miss Sophisticated," Shelley
harrumphed. It used to get to her when her
roommates bugged her about being from the
Midwest, but no more. She'd learned to accept their ribbing and even dish out some of
her own. At first, she'd felt a bit left out, living with Dana, a dyed-in-the-wool New Yorker

with not one, but two mothers because her parents were divorced, and with Faith, a street-wise Washingtonian whose police-officer father had been shot in the line of duty. Shelley couldn't even imagine family situations like theirs. She felt as if she'd been blessed with normality, but Faith and Dana acted just the opposite, as if she was the one who came from the moon. It had taken months to work things out among them, but now, different or not, the girls were inseparable.

"I love it!" Dana declared, staring at the new arrangement. She worked studiously at the angle of the table until it was just right. "I really think it's the nicest thing we've got. Maybe we should go antique all the way, redo the room entirely."

"Yeah, great. With what?" Shelley asked, getting up and coming over to admire the table.

"Mrs. Druyan is chucking out this horse-hair sofa," Faith commented. "It's really wonderful — except for the fact that it hurts to sit on it."

Dana giggled and picked up a pillow to toss at her roommate. "Then we can invite Ms. Allardyce in and threaten her. 'One more assembly, my fine headmistress,'" Dana rubbed her hands gleefully, "'and you'll be forced to sit on that sofa for three hours straight. See how you like it'"

"'That's real brilliant, Dana." Faith, ever

the practical one, was always sowing the seeds of doubt in Dana's hairbrained schemes. "Then she'll expel us and we'll have to go back where we came from and we won't be able to live together."

"Rotten idea," Shelley sighed, running a hand over the smooth, cool marble. "Guess we'll keep the decor the way it stands, then. Except," she added, walking slowly over to Dana's closet, "for this!" With a sweep of her hand, she opened the door, allowing sneakers, jogging clothes, and a variety of gloves and T-shirts to come spilling out into the middle of the floor.

"Wow!" Faith declared as Dana blushed in embarrassment. "What architectural style is this, Dana? Early Laundry Modern?"

Dana stared at the heap, trying to disown it. It refused to go away, but instead, sat there stubbornly for everyone to see. "All right!" she acknowledged. "Okay! I'll clean it out. Tomorrow."

"Today," her two roommates chorused.

Dana took a deep breath and dug in.

It was cold and raining when they got up the next morning to the sound of Shelley's digital electric alarm clock. The light through the batik curtains was hazy, barely visible. It was like seeing through a veil of fog.

"Oh, let's skip it," Faith sighed, digging further under the covers.

"No way." Shelley was already out of bed,

her mop of blonde hair the only bright thing in the room.

"Does Ms. Allardyce enjoy making us suffer?" Dana asked rhetorically as she rolled onto the floor and began doing her thirty daily sit-ups. "Does the sight of a few hundred girls who've been deprived of sleep make her heart sing?"

"I don't think she thinks about us," Faith grumbled. She opened one eye, then the other. "I think she's just wrapped up in her own little world — and Canby Hall's. We are the insignificant ants in the big hill."

It was true that nobody knew very much about Ms. Allardyce, and her background and personality were sources of constant contemplation for the girls. They knew she had a younger brother who'd been in a lot of trouble when he was a kid, because he'd shown up in Greenleaf several months ago. Ms. Allardyce had been totally hostile about even seeing him again, until she found out that he'd gone straight and was now a model citizen, someone any big sister could be proud of. But her initial reaction to him had been typical of her relationships with the students and faculty of Canby Hall — frigid to the core.

The girls shuffled out to the bathroom down the corridor, moaning and groaning as they went that they'd be last in line for one of the five showers anyway, so why should they even bother trying to get to the assembly on time? As luck would have it, there were two free stalls — only Dana had to wait.

"Boy, what a day." Heather, the floor monitor, stood barefoot on the tile floor, rubbing her eyes.

"Dana, do you know what this is about?" Casey Flint asked. Casey was the roommates' best friend aside from each other, and they were glad she was on their floor. She was a wry, cynical girl with more than a touch of mischief to her. Her parents were enormously wealthy art dealers who traveled on business more than they were home. With years of practice, Casey had gotten used to taking care of herself, and she was an expert at dealing with difficult situations.

"Not a clue," Dana shrugged. "I just hope it's not about morale or grades. Those are my two most unfavorite subjects."

"Personally," Ginny Weissberg said as she stepped out of the shower, a towel around her slim frame, "I think it's about posture. No more slumping at Canby Hall."

"That's not it," Casey declared. "It must be the food. We're going to take a vote on whether the cafeteria should be declared a toxic waste dump."

"I vote yes," Faith sighed as she left one of the stalls free for Dana. "Now can I please go back to sleep?"

As they were standing there talking, the door to the bathroom opened and in walked

Pamela Young, yawning delicately. Even when she'd just woken up, Pamela looked perfectly gorgeous. She had the kind of honey-blonde pageboy that *always* turned under exactly the same amount all the way around, and the kind of "sloppy" clothes that could have been displayed in a magazine ad. The reason for this was that Pamela's mother, Yvonne Young, was an international film star, and she spared no expense when it came to her daughter's wardrobe. The lovely looks and great clothes did nothing to improve Pamela's personality, however. The words "mean and nasty" had been invented just for her.

"What do you think the assembly's about, Pamela?" Ginny asked.

"The what? Oh, that." Pamela looked as if the topic were too insignificant to warrant her attention. She shrugged. "Who knows? Who cares? Anyone want to come to my room to see the most *divine* hand-painted silk underwear that Yvonne just sent me? She picked it up at this darling little shop on Rodeo Drive." She slipped out of her long, cotton kimono, revealing a totally unmussed embroidered muslin nightgown.

"Sounds nice," Heather nodded. "After the assembly."

"Are you guys really going to that stupid thing?" Pamela asked in amazement.

"Everyone has to go, Pamela. You know that," Faith told her.

"Well, too bad. They can come get me if they really want me that much." As Dana stepped out of the shower, Pamela swept in front of the three girls ahead of her in line and disappeared into the stall. The others just looked at one another.

At last, Shelley broke the silence. "Well, I guess it's time to start the day. Shall we?"

"Sure," Dana nodded.

"Okay by me," Faith declared.

The three roommates were ready by eight and pulled on their hats and parkas before scurrying down the stairs, into Baker's front hallway. Grumbling girls, few of whom saw any need at all for an assembly first thing in the morning, were already starting out into the rain. As Dana, Faith, and Shelley filed out behind the others, Alison joined them.

"It'll be short," she assured them as they splashed their way over to Main Building, just across the little park from Baker House. "I know Ms. Allardyce always calls a meeting of the administrative staff first thing Monday morning, so she can't keep us."

"What do you think it is, Alison?" Dana asked. "Grades, food, or steering clear of the Oakley Prep boys during exam week?"

Alison grinned. "I haven't a clue, honestly. But if we've heard the message before, I hereby give you all my permission to catch a few extra winks. I certainly intend to."

Laughing conspiratorially, they entered the

huge oak doorway of the building where most of their classes were held. The auditorium was just down the hall, and they trudged along with the girls from the other two dorms, Addison and Charles, into the large hall where they took seats in the back next to Ginny, Heather, and Casey.

Before everyone was even seated, the headmistress of Canby Hall appeared from stage left. She was dressed impeccably, as she always was, and her neat, champagne-colored chignon was pulled back so tightly, her gray eyes seemed to be spread even further apart than usual. Ms. Allardyce was wearing a beige linen dress with a wide black belt and black patent pumps. Dana had to admit, even though she wasn't awfully fond of Ms. Allardyce, that nobody except her own mother had clothes that could even begin to compete. Ms. Allardyce was a fashion plate, albeit a conservative one.

"Girls! Please!" Ms. Allardyce tapped the microphone that stood center stage, and feedback whined into the hall. Shelley and Faith covered their ears.

"Sorry about that." She fiddled with the head of the mike and put it in a new position on the floor. The sound stopped, and suddenly, everyone was silent, at attention.

"I want to thank you all for coming here so early this morning," Ms. Allardyce began in her quiet, low voice. She looked around the hall, attempting to take in every eye. "I

wouldn't have disrupted your day, had it not
been for the upsetting and urgent nature of
the following announcement."

There was a murmur through the auditorium. Clearly, this was not to be one of the
headmistress' typical pick-me-up speeches.
This was serious.

"I'll get right to the point. As you all
know," she went on, "Horace Canby estab-
lished this school in memory of his daughter,
Julia, in 1897 on the property that would
have been her inheritance. Had she not died
of fever while traveling in Europe, had she
lived into her teens, she would have attended
a school very much like this one, and Mr.
Canby wanted to be sure that her peers would
be entitled to the kind of education he would
have provided his daughter. In accordance
with Mr. Canby's request, over half the students who attend Canby Hall are here on part
or full scholarship. The estate and the grounds
have remained in the Canby family to this
very day."

"What's she getting at?" Dana whispered to
Shelley.

"I can't imagine." Shelley shook her head,
still staring at the tall woman who stood onstage.

"I don't like it, whatever it is," Faith murmured.

Ms. Allardyce cleared her throat and went
on. When she spoke again, her voice was
quiet, almost emotional. "What you don't

know is that there was no stipulation in Mr. Canby's will that this property should be used as a school *in perpetuity*. Those are the key words. I suppose he assumed that every Canby down the line would feel as he did about the education of young ladies, but in fact, this is not the case. The current Canby on our board of directors, Mr. Owen Canby, has informed me that he wishes to reconsider the use to which this property should be put. He feels — let's see, how did he put it? — that this institution is no longer financially viable. It is not a high-yield, growth investment, which is what he believes all of his assets should be. He has a very desirable buyer, a small corporation that has, until now, been stationed in Boston. The president is thinking of expanding his company. And, if the sale goes through, as Mr. Canby assures me it will, our school will close as of the end of this semester."

Everyone in the hall sat stupefied, paralyzed, turned to stone by Ms. Allardyce's frightful words. And then, quiet as the hall had been, it erupted in shouts of protest. Dana, Shelley, and Faith clutched each other. They stared at each other with tears in their eyes, trying to comprehend the fact that their world had just fallen apart.

CHAPTER TWO

"I won't be informing your parents until it's absolutely necessary," Ms. Allardyce continued when, at last, there was a semblance of order in the hall. "I did feel, however, that I owed it to you all to put you on alert."

Dana couldn't sit still another moment. She stood, her legs shaking with the realization of what was going to happen to her, to everyone in this room. "He can't do that!" she stated firmly.

"Right on!" Faith concurred.

"Oh, this is awful!" Shelley whispered to Alison.

"I'm afraid he can, my dear," Ms. Allardyce said sadly. "We have no endowment, as other schools have, and the Canby money can be used any way the current heir sees fit."

"But we ought to have more time," Mr. Washburn, one of the English teachers, demanded. "This doesn't sound legal, to close up a deal like this so soon. Surely there should be a hearing."

"There's already been a legal hearing on the matter, John," Ms. Allardyce told him. "I did everything I could. . . ." Her voice trailed off, and for a moment, the steely exterior of this determined woman seemed to melt.

"When should we — ? Is there anything we can do?" Casey called out.

Patrice Allardyce looked around the room once more. She paused before saying, "I would be most grateful for any of your suggestions, of course. But I can't hold out much hope. It's pretty well decided."

Again, the room was deathly still. Finally, Ms. Allardyce walked offstage, and everyone understood that the assembly was over. Slowly, one by one, girls and teachers began to get up and walk out.

"This is absolutely unbelievable." Alison, who'd been sitting with her hands over her face, suddenly slapped the seat in front of her and stood up, a look of fury on her attractive face.

"Let's call a meeting," Dana said impulsively. "All of Baker. We should talk about it."

"Good idea," Faith nodded, already halfway up the aisle. "If we put our heads together, I'm sure we can think of something."

"Sounds like Mr. Canby's already a hundred steps ahead of us," Shelley said dismally.

"But we can't give up without a fight!" Dana told her, pushing her along toward the door. "We won't!"

They raced back through the now-pouring rain, stopping other girls from the dorm as they went. By the time they got back to Baker, they had a contingent of desperate and iron-willed teenagers, all ready to do battle for the school they sometimes cursed, sometimes blessed, but always depended on.

"C'mon, into the lounge!" Alison corralled her charges into Baker's oak-paneled room, then rushed around turning on the antique brass lamps. The day had been dark to begin with, but now, after the news, it seemed positively black.

"Is everybody here?" Dana asked, scouring the room. Girls were sitting on the overstuffed sofas and armchairs, and those who hadn't found a place were sprawled on the oriental rug that covered most of the lounge floor. There were forty or so, Dana calculated, which meant that about ten girls were missing.

"I think Pamela went to the dining hall," Mary Beth Grover stated. She was a thin girl with a white, pinched face who hung around with Pamela because she thought it gave her prestige.

"Well, forget her," Dana shrugged. "Where's Ginny and Ellie?"

"I saw them on their way to their first

class," Faith told her. "Might as well start without them." The three roommates had somehow, without discussing it, decided to run this meeting. They stood together like the Three Musketeers, near the long, leaded-glass windows that were now streaked with rain.

"Okay," Shelley said, "who wants to talk first?"

"Me," Alison said. She was standing by the door with her arms folded, and even in the dim light, everyone could see that her hazel eyes were glistening with unshed tears. "I've been at this school now for four years, ever since I graduated from college. I feel it's been a rare privilege to work here, to know you girls and the ones who came before you. There's a special spirit about this school, something very precious. I can't tell you how this news breaks me up." Then she stood up straighter, slamming one fist into her other hand. "Let's go see this Canby person. Let's talk to him."

"I don't know about that, Alison." Joan Barr, sitting on the floor with her arms wrapped around her knees, had an air of quiet authority. "We have to have a plan. Something that'll convince him that we can become a . . . a high-yield, growth investment. Just going and pleading for a reprieve isn't going to do it."

"What about a bake sale?" Eileen Davis, a

tiny sophomore with more energy than a tornado, was on her feet and moving restlessly around the room.

"Are you kidding?" Cheryl Stern was practically rolling on the floor.

"That's the dumbest thing I ever heard," Casey said flatly. Most of the girls in the room were either giggling or looking at poor Eileen disparagingly.

"Leenie, do you realize how many cookies we'd have to sell to raise enough money for an endowment?" Alison chided softly.

"The entire town of Greenleaf would have to eat itself sick for the next decade," Dana pointed out. "Not a very feasible idea, Eileen." Dana rolled her eyes and looked heavenward.

"But it was a nice try," Shelley said comfortingly, attempting to make Eileen feel better. Shelley always went out of her way to try to repair hurt feelings — she was that kind of person.

"Anyone else?" Faith asked, looking from one girl to the next. "Think of what's at stake here, folks — c'mon!"

"I have a thought," Cheryl said pensively, her dark brown eyes intense and determined. "Do you think we could find another building in town for Mr. Canby? Maybe the corporation would agree to buy something other than Canby Hall, like an old bank or an office complex."

"But Owen Canby doesn't stand to make a

penny from the sale of another building," Dana told her. "It's our school that's in his family's possession — nothing else."

There was silence as everyone racked their brains. A couple of throats were cleared, a couple of people said, "Well. . . ." Then more silence.

"Oh, someone must have a good suggestion," Shelley sighed, anxiously twisting the gold bracelet she wore around her right wrist and never took off, not even for showers. Her boyfriend Tom had given it to her for her birthday, and every time she touched it, she thought of him. If she had to leave school and go back home to Iowa, she'd probably never see him again. "We're not dummies — you can't be stupid if you go to Canby Hall!"

"We could write a letter to the Massachusetts Board of Education," Casey suggested.

"Saying what?" Faith prodded.

"You know, registering a complaint. Is this school under the Board of Education's jurisdiction?"

"Yes," Alison nodded. "But the property the school is on is privately owned. You can't get the state to twist Mr. Canby's arm. As a matter of fact," she laughed despairingly, "Mr. Canby sounds like the kind of man who probably *owns* a few members of the board."

"What do you mean?" Shelley asked. "How could he own them?"

"Oh, you know, the way a rich person gets to put people in his pocket, people who do favors for him in exchange for preferential treatment." Alison ran her fingers through her hair, thinking again. "This is tough," she said finally.

"What's the matter with all of us?" Dana cried. It suddenly occurred to her what the sale of Canby Hall would mean. She would go home to her mother and her sister Maggie on New York's Upper East Side, back to the local high school she'd attended for freshman year. She loved New York, but something important had happened to her since she'd been at boarding school, and she knew she'd never be the same again. Part of it had to do with Faith and Shelley, whom she didn't think she could live without, and part of it was fending for herself, living in a situation where she made choices and learned to discern the right ones from the wrong ones. She couldn't bear the thought of seeing all that dissolve before her eyes.

"Why are we standing here talking about it?" Dana asked the crowd. "We've got to *do* something, and fast. All right now, the assignment is for everyone to go away and come up with a scheme. I don't care how weird or how impossible, just work on it. We'll meet again tonight after dinner. Anyone you see from the other dorms, get them to come, too. How's that?" She glanced around, happy to see so many heads nodding in agreement. Shelley gripped her hand, giving her the kind of support she needed.

"Okay, that's all for now," Faith told them. "We better get to class or the school will be closed on grounds of academic incompetence!"

Everyone laughed a little at that, and then they all filed out, back into the rain. Faith followed her roommates and Alison out the door, thinking about her last comment. She joked about the demise of Canby Hall, just as she joked about a lot of stuff that bothered her. Not her family, of course. If she went home to them in June, maybe she'd have the time to get back to the closeness she'd had with her brother Richie and her sister Sarah. Since Faith had left home, it was as if they'd been wrenched apart. Richie would be a teenager himself soon — he'd need her there to show him the ropes. Since she'd come to Canby Hall she'd gotten to know different kinds of people, but there was something comforting about the notion of coming home, of being with family.

"Penny for your thoughts," Shelley said as they hurried toward their biology class across the birch grove in the science building.

"Oh, nothing. And everything," Faith laughed, splashing both of the others as she leaped into a puddle. Yes, home would be nice, but right now, the only important thing was saving Canby Hall. Family would always be there for her — friends might disperse like seeds thrown to the wind.

"Let's cut class," Dana suggested with a wicked glint in her eye. "We need the time to plan." When the others stared at her skeptically, she shrugged. "We can get the notes from Ginny. She never misses a thing. Besides, coming up with a way to save our school is a lot more important than Darwin's theory of evolution. Isn't it?"

Faith and Shelley nodded solemnly. They switched direction, hurrying around the overflowing wishing pool in the center of the park on their way to the library. When the weather was good, there were dozens of places on the beautiful old campus to go for pow-wows. In the rain and snow, however, the choices were limited.

They raced in the back entrance, past Michael Frank's office toward the staircase that led to the basement. Michael, the guidance counselor, was the only faculty member who might see them playing hooky, and they were counting on the fact that he wouldn't get them in trouble. Once, a while back, Dana had developed a painful crush on Michael, but she was well over it now, and they were friends. As for Faith and Shelley, they knew he was one grown-up who could always be trusted.

"The Round Table Room — that's always empty," Shelley told them. "Since we Thespians just started technical rehearsals for the spring play, we're not working in here anymore." She opened the door to the cavernous room, which had a small raised stage at one end and the legendary round oak table at the other, a piece of furniture so filled with memories and girls' carved initials, it was sacred to every actress who'd ever learned her lines sitting there. Shelley touched it with a kind of reverence as the three of them sat down and stared at each other.

"A plan," Dana said. "Where do we start?"

"Well, we need an endowment," Shelley declared. "Now, where can we get one of those?"

Faith snorted. "They don't grow on trees, Shel."

"I know that," she huffed indignantly. "But they're around. Other schools have them — Oakley Prep for one." Oakley was their brother school, a boys' academy just a half a mile down the road from Canby Hall. The two schools were similar in quality, and the kids were always having mixers and other extracurricular activities together. Both Faith and Dana had dated Oakley boys, and had rather bad experiences. Tom, Shelley's boyfriend whom she'd met through the Thespians, went to Greenleaf High, the local public high school, as did Johnny Bates, the boy Faith had been dating since last year. Randy Crowell, Dana's boyfriend, who was now more of a friend than a *boy*friend, graduated from Greenleaf High the year before. He now worked on his family's farm, the only job he ever wanted to have. He was away this winter, helping his father buy horses in Kentucky.

"You're right," Dana told Shelley. "Oakley

does have an endowment. So do Andover and Exeter. And then there's the Madeira School and some of the more exclusive girls' schools around the country. But what have they got that we ain't got?" she asked with false cheer.

The other two stared at her. "I don't know. What?" Shelley asked.

"Rich alumni. You have to have generations of old money, pull, connections."

Faith made a face at her. "Well, *my* family's old, but I'm afraid we can't help out in the connections category. I'm the very first Thompson to go to a private school."

"That goes for me, too," Shelley sighed. "And my parents were embarrassed enough at the thought of their daughter going East to school. I don't think they would have considered it if they hadn't been scared to death that I was going to quit entirely at fifteen and marry the boy next door."

"You wouldn't have married Paul then, would you?" Dana looked scandalized.

Shelley made a face. "I guess not. But I was pretty stupid before I came here, pretty naive. I still like Paul a lot — but I don't think marriage is in the cards. And of course, now there's Tom, too." Shelley was still managing to juggle two men in her life. This was considerably easier because one of them was a thousand miles away from the other.

"Hey, we're off the topic, folks!" Faith pointed out. "The endowment. How much *is* an endowment, anyway?"

Dana scratched her head. "I think Harvard probably has hundreds of millions — I know it's some phenomenal amount. I guess we should find out what Mr. Canby left, exactly."

"You know, I read something about Harvard a couple of months ago in *Boston* magazine. They never actually use the endowment, except when they endow a faculty chair for some special person," Faith said. "It's just supposed to be wisely invested so the financial wizards on the board of directors can use the interest the principal has earned to run the school."

"You mean, they go to all that trouble for money they never use?" Shelley asked, incredulous. "How dumb!"

"Well, it's paper money, like when you invest in the stock market. You know you have it — even though you can't touch it — just in case."

"I see," said Shelley, although she didn't.

"So the most important thing we have to find out is not really where to get an endowment, but the practical part. How much does it cost to run a school like this for a year? Let's see." Faith took the notepad Dana had just started scribbling on and did some quick calculations. "We've got two hundred fifty kids, right? The ones who aren't on any scholarship pay — what is it? — five thousand in tuition?"

"Are you kidding?" Dana scoffed. "It's eighty-five hundred. Every year! My folks told me, because they pay two-thirds of that and my scholarship takes care of the rest."

"Okay." Shelley motioned for Faith to start writing as she talked. "Suppose half the student body pays full price and the other half have some kind of partial deal, like us. That would make. . . ." She reached in her head for the numbers.

"A million and a half dollars . . . or so." Dana shook her head in disbelief. "Yikes! Is that right?" Quickly, she did the computation again. "It's right."

They all looked at each other, horrified by the implication of their figures.

"Well, you should be able to run a school on *that*," Shelley said decisively. "I certainly could."

"I don't know about that," Faith said hesitantly. "Don't you think, if you add up all the teachers' and staff's salaries, and lab equipment, and typewriters and paper and pencils, and the awful food they feed us, and the upkeep of the buildings and grounds, and the books and desks and lamps and replacement furniture. . . ." Faith ticked them off on her fingers. "That's got to be a lot more than just the money Ms. Allardyce gets from tuitions. I think we should tack on another million."

"We'll never do it," Shelley said miserably. "How can we possibly raise that much?"

Dana's face was set and excited. She had that determined look in her eye she always got when someone told her she couldn't do something. "We have to start canvassing the student body. That's what they do at the fancy schools. Every few months, they have a drive and they call up the alumni and beg and plead and lobby for money. So . . . who's got rich mothers who went to Canby Hall? Didn't Andrea Granick once mention that she was the third one in her family to grace these ancient halls?"

"Yes, I remember that," Faith nodded. "I also remember her saying that her father was the world's greatest tightwad. Do you know she's the only girl in Baker House who has *no* allowance for extras like records and movies?"

"So she's out." Shelley got up and paced the room, then walked to the stage and hoisted herself up onto it. "I think Toni Eberhardt is rich. I'm not sure she had any family here, though."

"That's not important." Dana took the notebook and pen back from Faith and jotted down Toni's name. "And we'll try Cheryl. Her father comes to visit her in a Jaguar."

Faith grinned and shook her head. "Shucks, and my mom just has a little old Chevy Vega. Guess I don't fit in."

Dana punched her shoulder. "You fit in like a piece of a jigsaw puzzle, you nut! Think of another!"

Faith laughed and snapped her finger. "Bingo! Why didn't we think of it before? Pamela Young! Her mother has made zillions of popular movies all over the world and she lives in that mansion in Beverly Hills when she's not in her villa on the Costa del Sol." Faith grinned at the others. "Of course, my family always vacations in Uncle Joe's backyard, but the Youngs seem to prefer Nice and Majorca, for some unfathomable reason."

"Hey," Dana said, giving her friend a playful poke. "Let's not get snippy, shall we? Not if we're about to ask Pamela for a few hundred thou."

"Well, there's only one problem there," Shelley sighed, "and that's Pamela's avowed hatred of tradition, school, us, and everyone and everything that has anything to do with Canby Hall. Why would she agree to ask her mom to fund us?"

"Miracles do happen," Faith said, getting up from the table. There was a glimmer of hope on her face now. "I'm going to try it."

"Okay," Dana said. "But we better not count out other possibilities. Anyone else?"

"How about somebody who didn't go to school here?" Shelley suggested in a flash of eagerness. "How about a Greenleaf banker or businessman, somebody who'd feel sentimental about our school?"

"Whew!" Faith let her breath out in a rush. "He'd have to be pretty mushy to put up *that* kind of dough."

"I'm going to call Tom as soon as he's home from school," Shelley said, jumping off the stage and starting for the door. "He knows everyone in town."

They both looked at Dana, then, but she seemed less enthusiastic than either of them. "I'll go for a run after classes . . . see if I can dredge up another solution out of this feeble brain of mine." She glanced down at her watch. "Guess we should show up at English. If we skip any more classes, we'll be docked and we won't be able to work on our brilliant ideas."

The three girls trudged out of the library, waving briefly to Michael Frank as they passed his office. The guidance counselor, who, like everyone else, had heard Ms. Allardyce's news that morning at the assembly, looked about as depressed as any girl who'd ever come to him with her problems.

"Don't worry, Michael," Shelley said under her breath as they made their way to the library door. "We're going to save our school — just you wait!"

CHAPTER THREE

Dana pushed her long, dark hair under a sweatband, pulled up her hood against the late winter chill, and started off, down the path from Baker House toward the sports complex, then left past the tennis courts and once around the skating pond. The bare branches glimmered with just a hint of frost, the old snow lying in clumps and heaps everywhere. If only a few buds would show on the trees! Even their presence gave Dana just a bit of hope — when the buds appeared, that meant the warm weather would follow . . . eventually.

She loved running. Just the thought of pounding down a dirt road, her long legs loping along as her arms swung evenly and surely, made her feel good. There was something cleansing about the activity, something she couldn't get from talking to friends or reading a good book. She liked to think of herself as an athlete gone wrong — or maybe an architect with muscle. Either way, she could think better while running. If her teachers would let her jog during exams, she'd probably ace every test.

She left the school property then, running out Old Fort Road toward the wild flower ridge. It would still be bare except for a few brown weeds, but that didn't matter — it was her favorite thinking spot, high up above the valley where Greenleaf sat like a frog in a pond, its neat houses and stores just dots on the far horizon. She dashed to the top, panting, and looked around. It was so lovely up here!

As she gazed at the landscape, she was astounded to find that there were tears in her eyes. She blinked them away, feeling that it was silly to be so nostalgic for a place, even before she knew for a fact that she'd have to leave it. She was such a city kid, and the streets of New York had always been her turf. Now, however, she knew the meaning of the hush of nature, of the peace of mind you could get by just being silent for a while and listening to the rustle of branches, the rush of a burbling stream, the drone of a bumblebee.

"This is nerd-y!" she exclaimed. "What I need is an idea, not a bunch of feelings!" Without pausing for breath, she started off again, not allowing herself the luxury of being touched by all this beauty. What she needed was a plan, and she needed it fast.

She ran down the ridge, then turned left toward Sheltok, the next town south of Canby

Hall. There was no traffic, so she jumped off the dirt path and took the road in order to make better time. Running fast was even better than jogging leisurely when it came to thinking things out.

"Mo-ney," she huffed. "Save the school. En-dow-ment. High yield." She squeezed her eyes shut, and she puffed this little chant as though she were one of a battalion of tired foot soldiers struggling back to camp.

"Uff! Ow!" She collided head-on with a wall of sweaty muscle and rebounded off, careening into the mud on the side of the road.

"I'm terribly sorry," the wall said, offering a hand to help her up. "I really didn't see you as I came around that curve. Boy, are you a mess."

Dana looked into a pair of the darkest hazel eyes she'd ever seen, and then beyond to the wild shock of red hair that sat in an unruly bush on top of her collision's head. He was wearing a huge grin, and two big dimples appeared in his thin cheeks when he smiled. The fringe of dark lashes that outlined those huge eyes belied his fair complexion.

"Are you okay?" he said when she didn't speak.

"What? Oh, sure. I don't mind a little mud." She really was filthy, she realized as he pulled her up. And as she put up a hand to push the hair out of her face, she felt a smear of the brown ooze on her forehead, as well.

"Are you Canby, by any chance?" he asked in a low, husky voice. "You seem like you might be."

"I am," she nodded. "How'd you know?" As she took a step back toward the path, she felt a wrench of pain in her left knee that took her breath away.

"Hey, you better sit down for a sec." He maneuvered her over to a fallen log and sat her down. "Want me to take a look at that?" he asked. "I had a first-aid course last summer when I went on a rafting trip in Colorado."

"I don't think there's anything wrong with it," she shrugged, gingerly pulling up the leg of her sweat pants. The skin on her knee was scuffed off, but there was no blood. She worked the leg back and forth a bit to make sure it was still functioning.

"I don't know how I know," he said, answering her last question. "Canby girls have a certain something — indefinable but nice." He gave her a wry smile.

"Dana Morrison," she introduced herself, putting out a grimy hand. "Are you Oakley?"

"You guessed it. But I'm new — a transfer student. My dad thought it might be a good idea for me to spend my senior year around the Boston area so I could interview at all the colleges around here. I was at Exeter last year — pretty stiff, let me tell you."

"I've heard. But Oakley's no breeze either."

She shook her head ruefully. "I'm afraid I'll be a transfer student next year — back home in New York."

"Oh, yeah. I heard about that. Your school's closing," he said matter-of-factly.

"Well, it's not closing yet!" she said, suddenly annoyed. "Nothing's really been decided. It's really just a rumor at this point."

The boy gave her a look of cynical disbelief. "It's no rumor, lady. It's a fact."

"Oh, it is?" She stood up indignantly and put her hands on her hips. "And what makes you such an expert?"

"I have inside information," he told her with another of those infuriating grins. "Oh, sorry. My name's Chris Canby."

"Chris what!?"

"Canby." He gave her a sly smile. "As in the school."

"You're . . . are you a relation?"

"One of the last," he told her. "My dad is the great-grandson of James Canby, who was Horace's older brother."

Dana was so excited, she could hardly speak. "Your father wouldn't be *Owen* Canby by any chance, would he?"

"The one and only," Chris laughed. "We're really a very small clan. There aren't many of us left."

"But. . . ." Dana didn't want to start an argument, but she had to know where this guy stood. If he was an ally, and she got friendly with him, maybe he could convince his father not to sell Canby Hall. Of course, there was a chance that he didn't know anything about it, in which case it might be possible for her to get him on her side from the very beginning. She hated to think of herself as a manipulative person, and normally she wasn't, but this was the opportunity of a lifetime — who was she to pass it up? And wait till Faith and Shelley heard about meeting Chris Canby!

"Well, I'm really pleased to meet you," she said. "You know, you learn all about how your school was founded and its traditions and everything, but somehow you don't connect living humans with all that ancient history. It's just such a shame. . . ." She let her words hang in the air, and a look of genuine sorrow shadowed her face. "I mean, your father must be a really important person, someone who believes in progress and education and all the really crucial things that make Canby Hall such an outstanding institution of secondary learning. Wouldn't you say?"

That sounds really dumb, Dana. You're pushing it.

"Well, actually," Chris said, crossing his arms across his broad chest, "he's not that interested in education, per se. What interests him is making money. He's quite good at it, too, I must say."

"But, well . . . money isn't everything," she said lamely.

"Now you're going to tell me that money

can't buy happiness, aren't you?"

"Of course. It can't. There are plenty of other important things in life, you know."

"Aha!" He had this maddening look on his face, like he'd had this argument many times before and had always won. "There *are* a lot of other things — you have a point. But if you aren't comfortable, if you can't feed your family and pay your rent, it's mighty hard to enjoy those other things."

"You know," Dana said, "you sound like you're about forty years old." She meant it as an insult, but he took it as a compliment.

"That's because I'm very mature for my age. And I've had a good teacher."

"Dad?" she said mockingly.

"That's the one. The best. He tells me that he's bringing the Data-Tech people over next week to take a look at the Canby Hall premises. Data-Tech is the company that's buying the estate — and for a terrific price. Dad told me all about it."

Dana just stared at him. "You don't really think that's the right thing to do, do you? After practically a century's worth of girls have come through those hallowed portals and made something of themselves as good, upstanding American citizens, you don't think that denying us a fine education for the sake of a few bucks is right, do you?"

"I certainly do. Dana, times have changed an awful lot since Horace Canby hired a few teachers and put up a couple of dormitories.

And if he were alive today, I'm sure he'd agree with Dad. You have to make some sacrifices here and there on the road to the future," Chris pontificated. "That's progress. That's the big truth of the world of high finance."

She scratched her head, examining this tall young man who stood before her, as though he were some kind of peculiar machine. "You're serious, aren't you? That's terrible. I'm really sorry for you."

"Sorry? Hey, listen. My family's doing all right. I get along beautifully with my dad; I've got all the allowance I could want; the stocks I've invested in are doing great; and I'm probably going to Harvard next year. You don't have to feel sorry for me," he laughed.

"But Chris. . . ." Dana was at a loss. She didn't know anybody — except maybe Pamela Young — who was so set and smug about material things. "Don't you and your father ever — oh, I don't know — don't you ever just feel like forgetting about how your stocks are doing and going to a ball game?" She was grasping for straws, and she knew it.

"Sure we do. We've got season box seats behind home plate for the Red Sox. Maybe, some day," he added with a wink, "I'll show you where it is. I mean, I'll take you."

"I sit in the bleachers whenever I go to a game," Dana said huffily. "Maybe I'll take *you* and show *you* what it's like."

He grinned, and she tried not to notice how nice his smile was because she was determined to dislike this guy. Still, she hadn't given up on him as a possible conduit to his father, so it was conceivable that she would have to see him again. She might despise his values, but he was still a person to be reckoned with.

"Tell you what," he said. "We'll do something my way once, then we'll try your way. Is it a deal?"

"A deal." She stuck out her hand and they confirmed the verbal agreement with a firm handshake. "Well, I've got to get back before I really freeze up."

"I'll run part way with you. Looks like those legs of yours really know how to put on speed."

She was abashed to realize that she was blushing. "I'd sort of prefer to jog alone today. I've got a lot on my mind that I have to think out."

"I can respect that," he shrugged. "But I'll be calling you, Dana Morrison. Maybe we can have another financial and economic discussion at Pizza Pete's sometime."

"Maybe," she said as she ran off, pulling up her hood and wanting to kick herself for having made so little progress with him. Then she laughed. Progress — that was the Canbys' favorite word, the banner they flew before the world. As for Dana, she preferred her antiquated notions and her antique marble table. Her mother always told her that it was the way of the world for one person to believe one thing, and another, something else. That's what made horse races. Only this time, Dana wished with all her heart that she and Chris Canby were both betting on the same pony.

"Well, what did you come up with?" Faith asked as they moved their trays down the line in the dining hall that evening. They could feel a palpable buzz in the air, as all the girls at all the different tables discussed their various strategies.

"You're never going to believe this," Dana began. Then she stopped, fascinated by the sight of Shelley dishing out a strange combination of cauliflower, lima beans, corn, peas, and pimentos covered with an unknown sauce onto her plate. "You aren't really going to eat that, are you?"

"Uh-uh. Wouldn't dream of it. I'm just taking it so I can send a sample to Ripley's Believe It Or Not. So what won't we believe?" Shelley demanded. They took their trays and started across the hall to a free table right by the long, floor-to-ceiling windows.

"I met Owen Canby's son when I was out running," she told them. "He's Oakley."

Faith dropped her fork. "How totally perfect! That's wonderful!"

"Oh, Dana, you're a genius!" Shelley exclaimed. "That's exactly the kind of pull Alison was talking about. And now we've got it!" She clapped her hands in sheer delight.

"Hold on — not so fast." Dana shook her

head. "The only kind of pull this guy is going to give us is in the opposite direction. He's a real chip off the old block, a carbon copy of his father. I've never met anybody so . . . so Republican!"

Shelley frowned at her roommate. "Dana," she said with a warning in her voice. "My whole family is Republican, and always has been."

"I'm sorry. I didn't mean that. It was just the first word that came to mind. What he really is, is devoted to the almighty dollar, and he watches the stock market the way most kids watch video games. Can you imagine anyone our age doing that?" she asked them incredulously.

"Not really," Faith said. "So we're back to zero," she sighed. "Except for Pamela."

"No, I don't think so. This Chris person said he wants to see me again, and even though I'm going to hate every minute of it, I'm going out with him. I know I can change his mind — I have to."

"And I have a date with Tom tomorrow afternoon at Pizza Pete's," Shelley said. "We're going to make a list of everyone in town who might be a possibility." She looked at them hopefully. "So that's something."

The girls ate for a while in silence, each thinking her own thoughts. The food, usually tasteless, seemed particularly bad that night, and eventually all three of them pushed away their plates and just stared at each other.

"Time to hit the books," Faith decided, getting up and taking her tray.

"Right." Dana and Shelley followed her over to the tray return and then strolled pensively back toward the dorm. Every evening from seven-thirty to nine-thirty they had Study Hours, and every Canby Hall girl was expected to be in her room, doing her homework. Tonight, however, not much work got done. Dana, Shelley, and Faith sat at their respective desks, just gazing out into space, wondering where in the world they were going to come up with a solution to their gigantic problem. Things looked pretty rotten.

CHAPTER FOUR

Shelley signed out on the clipboard attached to the door of Room 407 as soon as she heard the *zoom* of Tom's motorcycle in the drive. Any time a Canby Hall girl left the premises, she had to sign out and sign in again — to prevent missing persons, Alison said.

Shelley raced down the stairs, grabbing her heavy gloves and the knitted cap that she'd been wearing this winter whenever she went out with Tom. It was the only piece of head-gear she owned that would fit under a motor-cycle helmet.

"Hey, I didn't even get a chance to knock!" Tom said as she ran out the door of Baker House straight toward him. He removed his own helmet, revealing his neatly cropped blue-black hair. Nobody in Iowa, Shelley had told Faith and Dana when she first met Tom, had hair even approaching this dramatic color. But of course, Shelley was slightly biased. She was nuts about Tom, and everything about him was extraordinary, according to her.

"I'm in a hurry — didn't want to wait," she gasped, putting out her arms for a hug. Tom pressed her to him, and the top of her head rested neatly on the breast pocket of his leather jacket — he was that tall.

"Did you make a list?" she asked as he unstrapped the other helmet and handed it to her.

"I've got everyone in town who might conceivably listen to a plea for money, and my dad and mom looked it over, too. By the way, Shel, they're real sorry to hear about all this."

She nodded, too preoccupied to be grateful for any kind of consolation. She climbed on board behind him, threw her arms around his waist, and they were off, flying down the drive and then out the main gates. The wind in Shelley's face was cold, but she didn't mind. She was just happy to be doing something — anything — that might lead to an end to their worries.

"There's someone I want you to talk to at Pizza Pete's," Tom yelled to her over his shoulder.

"What? Can't hear a word!" Shelley screamed over the noise of the engine.

"Cary Sampton. Mr. Sampton's lived in Greenleaf all his life, probably since the town was just a lot of farms grouped around a general store. He knows everybody, and he always has Tuesday dinner at Pizza Pete's because of the senior citizen discount."

"Who?" Shelley had caught maybe every other word. Something about a Mr. Sampton.

"Never mind. Later," Tom chuckled. Then he revved the engine and drove on.

They were at the center of Greenleaf in about ten minutes, instead of the twenty minutes it took to walk swiftly from Canby Hall. Luckily, Tom was a *slow* motorcycle driver, unlike some of his nutsy friends at Greenleaf High. He parked the cycle in front of the stationery store, climbed off and gave Shelley a hand down.

"Cary Sampton," he repeated as they walked toward the pizza parlor. "He's the man who can help us. He's kind of a hermit, a rough old codger, but believe me, Shel, he's the person to ask. He may seem like sandpaper on the outside, but inside, he's just as soft as a bowl of jelly."

Shelley tried to imagine a man made of jelly covered with sandpaper, but it was useless. Sometimes, Tom's comparisons made no sense at all.

"Hi, kids, what'll it be?" Sally, who'd been a waitress at Pizza Pete's as long as anyone could remember, was at their table with menus and glasses of water even before they sat down.

"Large sausage and mushroom, Sal, with

extra cheese," Tom said expansively. Then he reached across the table and took Shelley's hand. "You wouldn't have to go home if Canby Hall closed, you know. You could finish up at Greenleaf High, with me. With my sister away at college, there's plenty of room in our house. Honest, Shel, my mom would love to have you. Not to mention me," he smiled warmly. Then he saw the look on her face. "I didn't mean to assume your school was closing, you know. I just meant you could have a place to stay."

"I know, Tom." Shelley squeezed his hand. He was so sensitive, so super-aware of her feelings.

She was touched by his invitation, but she didn't know how to respond. She liked Tom so much — sometimes, she thought she loved him — but it was terribly confusing. Paul, her old flame, was back in Pine Bluff, still writing her letters that said in no uncertain terms that he hadn't stopped praying and hoping that she was still his girl, regardless of all the miles and experiences that had come between them. Paul had come to visit her once and had actually met Tom, and the whole thing had set Shelley's mind whirling. What *did* she want, really? Was it home and hearth and becoming a farmer or storekeeper's wife? Not anymore. Was it a life on the stage, the kind of existence Tom was always going on about? She wasn't sure. And these days, she wasn't even sure what she wanted for lunch or dinner. Living with Tom's family would be wonderful, in a way, but it might be awkward. She couldn't accept.

"Well, you're absolutely marvelous to ask me," she said at last. "But we don't really have to worry about that yet, do we? I mean, the sale hasn't gone through, and Dana and Faith and I are working night and day on a scheme to raise lots of money." She bit her lip, thinking about the exact amount they had to come up with. "Do you know that we figured that all the tuitions together, even counting the scholarship students, equal about a million and a half dollars? Per year?"

"Wow! And that's nowhere near what it costs to run the school, either."

Shelley took her hand out of his and stared. "What do you mean?"

"I don't know exactly, but a private school's budget is a whole lot more than the sum of the tuitions. I just know because of my sister's college. But how could you raise that much?"

Shelley frowned, shaking her head as Sally proudly brought their pizza, piping hot, to the table. "I haven't the foggiest."

"Dig in, kids," Sally grinned. "What am I saying? You guys don't need any instruction," she chuckled. "I've seen you put away more than one pizza in the past year and a half. Just remember to chew it, not inhale it." With that, she walked away to the next table, where an old man wearing a pork-pie hat and a baggy, blue-knit cardigan with elbow patches was drinking a cup of soup and turning the pages of the Greenleaf *Chronicle*, the local paper.

"That's him! That's Mr. Sampton," Tom said.

"Oh, him. Sure, I've seen him around a lot," Shelley concurred. She tried not to look obvious as she glanced over at the man, who was now slicing his pieces of pizza neatly in half. "I have a feeling there's more sandpaper than jelly there," she noted, watching his bushy gray eyebrows dance in annoyance as he sawed away at the gooey cheese. "How well do you know him?" she asked.

"Not very, but then, nobody does. He lives in a log cabin he built himself, way out by the edge of town. I know he still farms a little, but he keeps pretty much to himself. The only reason he comes to town is to buy supplies and to get a cheap meal here. Well?" He wiped his mouth with a napkin and pushed his chair back. "Shall we beard the lion in his den? Or should I say lioness?" This was Tom's attempt at a joke, since the lioness was Canby Hall's mascot.

Shelley shook her head. "Let's wait till he finishes eating. It's not polite to interrupt." One thing her mother had drummed into her from earliest childhood was manners. "Show me your list."

Tom shrugged and produced a piece of yellow legal paper from his back pocket. There were about ten names on it, some followed by question marks. "Mr. Johansen runs Greenleaf Savings and Loan, and Mr. Tyler's the president of Greenleaf Federated Trust. I only know them by sight. Then there's Dr. Antman, and Mom swears he gives a lot of money to charity every year. I don't think Scott Rowlands is a very good bet, but he's down anyway, and so's Abel Pease. Those two are arch enemies, so if one gives, the other might chip in about a dollar more just because they're such rivals. But Shel, we're talking probably hundreds — at most — from each of these guys. I don't know how you're ever going to approach a million."

"More — that's what you said." She took the list and stuck it in her pocket, hardly even glancing at it. "Look, Mr. Sampton's just starting his coffee. Now!" She got up and rather shyly walked over to the old man's table, Tom following behind her.

"Ahem." She cleared her throat, but Mr. Sampton didn't even look up from his paper. "Um, excuse me, sir," she said. "Would you mind very much if we sat down?".

"Plenty other chairs free," Mr. Sampton growled. He finally cocked his head, looking up at her out of one rather beady brown eye, rimmed with red. "Who're you?"

"I'm Shelley Hyde, and this is my boyfriend, Tom Stevenson. We go to school around here. I mean, not the same school. I go to Canby Hall and Tom goes to Greenleaf High, and. . . ." She stopped, seeing that he was clearly not interested in where they went to school, or even *if* they went to school. Mr. Sampton simply glowered at them, waiting for them to go away so he could finish his coffee.

Tom moved in a little closer and smiled at the irascible man. "Sir, I'm Joe Stevenson's boy. I hear you knew my grandfather, Frank. He was a blacksmith in his younger days; worked up near the old mill. Then he went into the hardware business."

"Sure, I knew him. Owed me twenty dollars for years on a bet. Finally paid off, though. Good man." Mr. Sampton, having made his pronouncement on Frank Stevenson, turned his back on them. Shelley looked at Tom despairingly.

"We really wouldn't bother you, sir, but we have a problem, and we thought you might be able to help us," Tom said quickly.

"Me? Help you?" The man was incredulous.

"You see, my school's in real financial trouble," Shelley burst in. "And Owen Canby is going to sell it to some company and we'll all have to leave Greenleaf. But we girls figured that if we could raise the money to keep it going for just another year, Mr. Canby might see that it was a . . . financially viable institution, and let it continue to exist just as it has up to now."

"And we thought, since you've lived here so long, you might be able to give us the names of Greenleaf people who might make a charitable contribution. Tax deductible, of course," Tom added.

"Ha! Most the folks I know in this town are skinflints — the lot of 'em wouldn't give you the time of day," he grumbled. "Now who's this Canby fella selling to?"

"It's a Boston corporation — I think Dana said it was called Data-Tech," Shelley told him. Was there a glimmer of interest in the man's eye, or was she just imagining it?

"Selling it to a corporation, is he?" Cary Sampton wagged a grizzled finger at them. "I know a few people who'd have something to say about that!"

"Right, sir," Tom continued. "Because one of the great things about living in Greenleaf is that it's a small, comfortable town. We don't want a lot of big-city strangers working and not living here."

But Mr. Sampton wasn't listening. He was busy scribbling away in a little spiral-bound notebook he'd taken out of his pocket. "When they planning to close you down, girl?" he asked without looking at her.

"By June, I guess. The end of the school year. It doesn't seem very far away," she added sorrowfully.

"Well," Mr. Sampton said, closing his notebook with a smart snap. "I can't give you any names. I don't pay attention to folks' financial status. But I tell you, I don't like the notion of a darn-fangled *corporation* moving in." His thick New England accent made it sound like *carp*oration. "I'm sorry for you, girl, that I am." He shook his head and, again, turned away, indicating that the audience was at an end.

"But can't you give us any suggestions at all?" Shelley begged. "We have to try everyone, just in case. Even if you think they'll say no."

"No," Mr. Sampton echoed. "But I'll give it some thought. You can always find me here, Tuesdays." He picked up his paper, moved his chair to face the wall, and buried himself in the sports section. Tom and Shelley slowly backed away, both of them totally befuddled by the old man's reaction. They left the money for their pizza and a tip on the table and walked out without a word.

They didn't speak until they were outside on the street, walking back to the cycle. Then Shelley said softly, "What a strange man!"

"I told you!" Tom grinned.

"Now what?" Shelley looked at him, her usually cheery face creased with concern.

"Well, as long as we're in town, why not try a few of the guys on the list? The banks are closed, but Dr. Antman's right across the street."

"You mean" — Shelley gulped — "go ask him for money?"

Tom put his hands on his hips. "Well, isn't that the point of this exercise?"

"Sure, but. . . ." She looked at the wooden office door with the words, *Jonathon Antman, M.D., P.C.* on a brass plaque beside it. "It's just . . . my mother always told me it was rude to ask people for donations."

Tom threw up his hands. "You want an endowment or don't you? Swallow your pride, girl, and go knock on that door."

The nurse saw them into the reception room, which was almost empty at that time of day, with only a couple of patients left. "May I help you?" the nurse asked.

Shelley nodded, feeling her nails digging into the palms of her hand. "We'd like to see the doctor, please. Oh, we're not sick or anything." When the nurse looked puzzled, she added, "It's a drive for our school."

"Hmm," was the nurse's skeptical response. "Just have a seat. He'll be with you when he has a free moment."

The free moment didn't come for another forty-five minutes, during which time Shelley and Tom read every magazine on the table and counted the number of paintings on the wall at least ten times. Finally, just as they were about to leave, the door to the inner office opened, and a large, beaming man with a shiny bald head and a white coat appeared.

"Come in, you two," he offered. "Got just a second, now."

"We won't be long at all," Shelley told him, feeling really stupid and totally unlike the great Canby Hall salesperson she was supposed to be. "It's about our school having to close," she began as he closed the door behind them.

Twenty minutes later, they walked out of the office, Shelley proudly bearing a signed check. She was shell-shocked, completely unable to speak. She'd hardly had a chance to explain the situation and plead her cause when the doctor took out his checkbook and started to write. She was so unprepared, she didn't have one slip of paper to use for a receipt, so he tore off a piece of his prescription pad for her to sign.

"It's unbelievable," Shelley muttered as Tom steered her toward his motorcycle. "I mean, could it really be this easy? Could I just go from house to house and tell everyone in Greenleaf what I told Dr. Antman?"

"Remember, sweetie, he's got a reputation as a philanthropist. I don't think you'd have the same kind of luck everywhere. So what'd he give you, anyway?"

Shelley giggled, realizing that in all the excitement, she hadn't even bothered to glance at the check. She opened the little envelope and pulled it out. As deliriously happy and elated as she'd been a second ago, she was now completely crestfallen. It was a check for a hundred dollars.

"Well, at least he gave something," Tom said consolingly.

"Right. One hundred dollars down; only nine-hundred, ninety-nine thousand to go," Shelley sighed. Then she raised her fists to the heavens and shook them — hard.

CHAPTER FIVE

Faith had been lying in wait for an hour, and she was getting fed up. Pamela always and unfailingly came down to the exercise room in the gym to work out at three o'clock. But today, of course, she was late.

Faith paced the wooden floor, thinking out her speech. She decided she would be straightforward and direct and say what she had to say. She would make it seem as though there was no other alternative for the school, and explain that the whole future of Canby Hall hung on Pamela's mother's shoulders. She'd *guilt* her into it! The only problem was, she didn't know whether Pamela, the only girl she'd ever met who had ice water running through her veins, had ever felt guilty in her life.

Johnny would know how to handle this, she thought. She'd been seeing Johnny Bates pretty steadily since last year, and she trusted him implicitly. He was reliable, steady, intelligent, handsome, and even though he did have ambitions to become a detective — a profession that spelled Danger with a capital D for Faith — she loved him dearly. He was a junior at Greenleaf High, and he helped out occasionally at his father's gas station, right in the center of town. Faith and Johnny had both been deluged with work for the past week and had simply been too busy to get together, but this would be a perfect time to call and get some advice.

Just as she started to the door, determined to corner Pamela the very next morning in the bathroom, the door opened and in walked the person in question, wearing a perfectly color-coordinated pink leotard with gray piping and gray tights with pink polka-dots. Her smooth cap of blonde hair was tied back with a pink ribbon. Faith couldn't help but smile. Pamela was the prime example of someone who was always all dressed up with nowhere to go.

"Hi!" Faith pretended to puff as she bent down to touch her toes. She wanted to give the impression of having been here all along, exercising.

"Oh, I didn't know the room was taken." Pamela made a face.

"There's room in here for about twenty people, Pamela," Faith shrugged, going over to the small set of barbells that lay against the wall. Recently, she'd gotten into lifting weights — not really because she enjoyed doing it, but more in memory of her father, who'd always prided himself on his wonderful physical condition.

Pamela looked at the weights in Faith's hands with astonishment. "You shouldn't be fiddling with those things, dear," she said in a patronizing tone as she sat on the floor and touched her head to her slim, straight legs. "It's terrible when girls get all muscle-bound — so unattractive."

Faith was about to tell her in no uncertain terms that weight-lifting was for toning, not muscle-building, but decided that argumentativeness would get her nowhere, fast. Sweetness and light were her best weapons today. "You're probably right," she said, putting down the ten-pound weights. "It's really something, isn't it, that we have all this equipment right here. I mean, this school has *everything*."

Pamela gave a delicate little snort. "You've got to be kidding. Why, my old high school in Beverly Hills had a pool, sauna, and hot tub room, not to mention a full Nautilus set-up. This rinky-dink place is sadly lacking in the essentials."

"That's what I mean." Faith backtracked hastily. She felt like a tactical military expert, planning each step of the battle while the campaign was already in progress. "If only Canby Hall had the financial resources of other private schools, we'd have everything our hearts desired."

"Well, you won't have to worry about that long. From what I hear," Pamela smiled, "the cards are on the table. To mix a metaphor, the goose is cooked; the plug has been pulled." She leaned back, pushing on her palms and the balls of her feet, and made a perfect backwards arc with her body.

"But it doesn't have to be that way, Pamela. . . ." Faith rushed over to her, looking at her upside down. "If we all pull together, we can change Mr. Canby's mind."

"Why in heaven's name would we want to do that?" Pamela's laugh was strained, like the cheep of an angry canary. "If I have to spend another winter in this arctic climate, I'll probably die, or at least come down with a terminal case of dry skin. Anyway, I'm sure you must be anxious to get back to . . . to wherever you used to go to school." Pamela said this carefully, implying that black girls where she came from didn't attend private school unless they were closely related to Michael Jackson.

"I don't want to leave Canby Hall, Pamela — none of us do."

"By 'us' I take it you're referring to those two other patriotic souls you room with."

"Dana and Shelley would be heartbroken, but they're not the only ones," Faith persisted. "C'mon, Pamela," she went on, a little exasperated now, "you can't tell me there's not one good thing about this school."

"Hmmm. . . ." Pamela put a finger to her

lips and looked at the ceiling. "Yeah, the scenery's sort of picturesque, if you like that sort of Christmas-card effect all year long. But that's about it."

Faith refused to give up. She'd crack this tough nut yet! "What about the dances with Oakley, and Song Nights, and skating on the pond? What about having the neat things from the old Canby estate right here on the property, with apple butter from our own orchard's apples and the pancake festival with maple syrup from our own trees? You don't get that in California!"

"We can buy all those things at the shopping mall," Pamela said in a bored tone. "And as for our brother school, the less I see of those immature, unsophisticated Oakley boys, the better. And now, if you'll excuse me, I have work to do." She stood up and started swinging her arms around her body.

"You know what the problem is, don't you?" Faith continued, ignoring Pamela's lack of interest. "It's just money. Nothing but money. Mr. Canby wouldn't have dreamed of selling this property if we had an endowment, like other schools."

"Well, if Ms. Allardyce isn't running this funny farm in the black, then she probably *should* be closed down," Pamela grunted.

"It's not her fault. It's that Horace Canby didn't write his will properly. If he'd provided for the school in perpetuity —"

"But he didn't," Pamela stated. "And if

somebody doesn't shell out an awful lot of bucks, the current Mr. Canby's going to sell and get them someplace else. I don't blame him in the slightest."

"Suppose somebody did shell out some money, though." Faith was going great guns now. Pamela herself had led right into this subject. "If the parents, say, all chipped in what they could, we'd have the funds we needed to keep the school going for another year. And when Mr. Canby saw that we were self-sufficient, he'd leave us alone."

"Sure," Pamela scoffed. "And what parent's going to just throw away all that dough?"

Faith pretended to think a minute. Then she snapped her fingers. "Your mother could do it! I mean, it would be wonderful for her career, for her image. I can just see the headlines in the *Hollywood Reporter* now — 'Yvonne Young Turns Philanthropist, Saves School'. Wouldn't that be great? And tax deductible, too."

Pamela gave her a look of extraordinary scorn. "Why should my mother give any money to this crummy old school? She's got lots of better charities."

"But it's your school — she'd have a stake in keeping it going."

"One school's as good as another," Pamela shrugged. "I mean, as *bad* as another." She got down gracefully into a crouch to do some squat thrusts. "I don't think Yvonne much cares which one I go to — or where it is."

"But think of it, Pamela. Think of all we'd be missing. Senior year is really terrific, with the special privileges and events and parties, not to mention graduation ceremonies. After all, if Canby Hall shuts down, you'd have to start all over again meeting people and learning the ropes at some other school." Faith paused for a moment before saying slyly, "And your mother would have to go to all the trouble of finding another place for you." It was rumored that Pamela had been tossed out of her last three boarding schools for not studying and blithely failing every test. It had been hard to get her accepted at Canby Hall, and it might be harder still to get her in anywhere else.

And in fact, this statement stopped Pamela in her tracks. She swallowed hard, and Faith could see her thinking out her options. "Well, I don't know if I can convince her, or even if I should. But she's supposed to be around in the next couple of weeks. She said she'd come to see me before she leaves for Europe. She's shooting her next picture in Italy, you know," Pamela added proudly. "And it's not going to be any low-budget production like that dumb movie they shot on our campus. This is the real thing," she said. A few months back, a New York production company had rented the Canby Hall estate to film their latest picture, and some of the girls, including Dana and Pamela, had gotten bit parts.

"Well, that's terrific!" Faith clapped her

hands together in delight. "Please let me talk to her when she's here, Pamela. You don't have to do a thing — just introduce me again. I'm very persuasive," she grinned.

Pamela shrugged. "No skin off my nose," she said, going back to her exercises. "But I better warn you that Yvonne has a lot on her mind. She's probably not going to be very interested in something as dull and ordinary as this stupid place."

"Just let me at her," Faith said with determination. "I bet I can convince her how important this is."

"If you insist," Pamela sighed, turning her back on Faith and starting her jumping jacks. It was Faith's cue to leave the room, which she did, practically skipping as she left the other girl to her exercises and closed the door behind her. As she started down the hall, a smile as wide as the entire Canby Hall campus wreathed her face. This was it! She could do it! If Yvonne Young contributed, say, five hundred thousand and one of the bankers Shelley came up with would lend them a few more, they could probably pay off the loan with smaller donations from some of the other parents. And if they all worked extremely hard on a great letter to be sent to the alumnae, with follow-ups every year, they might be well on their way to a full endowment for Canby Hall. Which meant that they'd never have to worry about relying on some stingy old Canby relative again.

She couldn't wait to call Johnny now! He was always going on about what a great mind she had, and she usually shrugged in embarrassment when he talked about her super brainpower, but right now, she had to agree with him. Faith was so busy thinking happy thoughts as she started back down the path toward the dorm, she didn't see the man walking directly in front of her, carrying a large standing lamp. She walked smack into Michael Frank, and the lamp spun in his arms before landing on one side of its bronze base on the path. It clattered to a complete stop, the metal ringing loudly on the bricks.

"Oh, Michael, I'm really sorry!" She reached over to touch the lamp gingerly, a pained expression on her face. "If I broke it, I'll kill myself. I can't afford to pay for it."

"Doesn't matter. No harm done. It was busted already. I was on my way into town to drop it off at the repair shop. Whatever's the matter with it, you couldn't have made it much worse." The guidance counselor was smiling, and his brown eyes looked particularly sparkling because of the crinkles that appeared around them when he grinned. Everyone on campus generally agreed that Michael was not only gorgeous, he was also a terrific person. Apparently, Alison, the girls' housemother, thought so too, because she and Michael had been dating for several months now. They were discreet, but since they'd been unable to hide their feelings from a band of overly curious teenagers, they now acknowledged that *something* deeper than friendship was going on between them.

"What's up?" he asked her as he picked up the lamp again and they started off together. "You look surprisingly happy for someone who's been told her academic future is in utter turmoil." He sighed, and she could see how upset he was, despite his light tone.

"I think we may have a solution," she said knowingly. "Dana and Shelley and I are sort of heading the committee to save Canby Hall, see, and we're all kind of playing around with different ideas on how to raise money. *I* just got Pamela Young," she added with a wink.

"Whew! Now that you've got her, what are you going to do with her?" Michael asked. Pamela was not one of his favorite students.

"I mean, I think I can get her mother to contribute some money. All we need is about a million or so, give or take a hundred thousand." She looked heavenward, as if even uttering the dread sum was enough to call forth the wrath of the gods.

"Oh, is that all?" Michael looked puzzled. "Tell me, how did you come up with that amount?"

Faith told him, adding that all they were trying for was one year's budget, after which time, they hoped Mr. Canby would change his mind about selling the school.

Michael bit his lip. He looked very worried

now. "I'm afraid you're a little off on the figures, Faith. At our last faculty meeting, Ms. Allardyce passed out copies of the annual report. The budget to run this school is *three* million dollars — count 'em. That's per year," he added needlessly.

Faith's jaw dropped about a foot. She stood in the middle of the path, absolutely horrified. Here she'd thought she had the problem licked, and now it turned out that she'd barely scraped the tip of the iceberg. "You can't mean that," she pleaded.

"It's pretty terrible, I know," Michael concurred. "Ms. Allardyce mentioned that she was going to have to raise tuitions within the next couple of years, just to make ends meet. That was before Mr. Canby's bombshell, though." He shook his head, and his handsome face seemed to age before her eyes. "I hate the idea of looking for another job, let me tell you. I think this place is ideal, for faculty and students alike. Besides," he smiled, breaking into song, "I've grown accustomed to the food."

Faith could barely speak. Why hadn't she thought of requesting facts and figures before they started out blindly on this stupid scheme? Johnny was going to think she was a real dolt, and Dana and Shelley would be a lot more than disappointed when she told them. They were back to square one, or at least, to square one million. And, to look at it quite honestly, they might be way off when it came to charitable contributions. Maybe even rich people didn't donate that much.

"Hey, are you all right? Talk to me, Faith." Michael put down the lamp and gave her arm a little shake.

"Yeah, oh sure. I just feel like somebody added a ten-ton weight to my shoulders, is all." She looked down at her shoes, suddenly wanting to get back to the dorm and tell the others. There was a certain amount of comfort in shared misery. "I'll see you later, Michael," she said as she hurried past him. "I'm glad you told me, really. And I hope the lamp can be fixed."

She didn't care about the lamp, though. She didn't care about anything. The meeting with Pamela's mother loomed frighteningly before her, and for the first time, she wondered if they were biting off more than they could possibly chew. This wasn't just kid stuff, this was the world of high finance, something about which neither she, nor Dana nor Shelley had any inkling. With a heavy heart, she raced back to the dorm, the bearer of the worst news yet. She just hoped that this was the last straw. At this point, she really couldn't take another.

CHAPTER SIX

"Oh, you can't *mean* that!" Dana wailed, when Faith mentioned the horrendous figure.

"That's perfectly impossible," Shelley declared. "Michael must have got it wrong."

"He had the annual report — what more do you want?" Faith began to pace their room in annoyance. "We should have known it was higher than we guessed."

"But *that* much higher?" Dana threw herself down on her mattress, covering her eyes with her arm like a heroine in an old melodrama. "I have a terrible desire to call that dumb Chris Canby and tell him off for his father."

"What good's that going to do?" Faith sighed. She looked from Dana to Shelley and back again. "How about robbing a bank?" Her expression was absolutely serious.

The other two girls were staring at her when Casey Flint flung the door open and raced into the room, panting. "I've got it! You'll never believe how long this took me. But I *know* we can do it. We can get the million."

"Tell her, Dana," Shelley sighed.

"You tell her."

"Tell me what?" Casey looked disgruntled.

"It's three million, not one. Which means we have two thirds less of a chance to win this battle," Faith moaned.

"Nonsense," Casey grinned. "What's a few mill here or there? Believe me, I know money people. I *come* from money people. You haven't even asked to hear my idea."

"Okay, shoot." Dana wasn't very hopeful, but she trusted Casey.

"I did something constructive," Casey said. "I made a list of all the possible Fortune 500 companies that give charitable grants to institutions. You wouldn't believe what I had to go through to get the info." She grinned and shook Dana's shoulder. "Don't look so glum. Maybe we can get some gigantic corporation to sponsor us, like the way the Chubb Group does public television."

The others just looked at her, not wanting to criticize, and not daring to laugh. After a while, Shelley opened her mouth. "Maybe we can," she nodded. "And maybe we can't."

There was a light tap at the door, and then a voice asked, "Can I come in?"

"Sure, it's open," Shelley said.

Alison's face was about as long as theirs.

Her usually smooth reddish-brown hair was wild. She was wearing big, roomy, denim overalls, which made her slender frame look even smaller. At a quick glance, she would have passed for one of her own girls.

"Mind if I sit down for a sec?" she asked, plopping down on the floor anyway.

"Alison, we've just had some awful news." Dana rolled over and leaned on both elbows, her green eyes penetrating as she spoke. "It takes three million bucks to run this school for a year — can you imagine? And even with me meeting Chris Canby, and Shelley covering the banks and local merchants, and Faith having an intro to Pamela Young's mother, we're still about two and a half million behind. I don't know what we're going to do."

"I hate to pile on the heavy stuff," Alison said softly, "but Ms. Allardyce has already drafted a letter to the parents. I read it over Peggy's shoulder yesterday. That woman may be the most loyal secretary our headmistress ever had, but she's just as upset about all this as we are. She told me she's supposed to mail these little love notes as soon as Ms. Allardyce meets with Mr. Canby on Saturday.

"Oh, no!" Shelley covered her eyes, as if to shut out the finality of this.

"How totally rotten," Casey muttered.

"Saturday, huh?" Faith sat heavily on the floor beside Alison. "Doomsday. I don't know, I feel like it's all over before we've begun. If we only had a little —"

"Where's the meeting, Alison?" Dana interrupted. She was alert now, and there was a glimmer of a smile behind her eyes.

"At Ms. Allardyce's house. Two o'clock, Peggy said."

"Great," Dana grinned. "I'm not doing anything on Saturday. Are you, Faith?"

Faith sat there for a second, and then the light dawned. "Not me. Not a thing. How about you, Shel? Casey?"

"Now just a second." Alison caught the drift of their intention before Shelley could speak. "Nobody invited you guys."

"This is an emergency, Alison," Dana stated. "And it requires drastic measures. We're not going to embarrass Ms. Allardyce — we're just going to be there for support. There can't be anything wrong with standing behind our fearless leader, can there?"

"Besides, it'll be five against one," Shelley grinned. "And there's strength in numbers."

"Oh, no, you're not getting *me* involved in this. I work here, remember?" Alison picked herself up and started for the door. "And if she asks where you got the information about this meeting, mum's the word, understand? Otherwise, I'll set the dogs on you."

"You have a cat, Alison," Faith pointed out. "And Doby couldn't hurt a flea."

"Oh, yeah?" Alison searched their faces, and finally relented. "Okay, you can go. And I wish you all the luck in the world. But kids," she added, "don't get your hopes up. I'm afraid it's all over but the counting." As she opened the door to Room 407, she winked at them. "Give it to them!" she instructed, before walking out.

It didn't take long for them to corral the staunchest members of the Save Canby Hall Committee. By dinnertime that night, Joan Barr, Cheryl Stern, Ginny Weissberg, and about eight others had promised to be at the headmistress' house promptly at two on Saturday. Each one vowed to come up with a list of persuasive points they could mention if Ms. Allardyce gave them a chance to speak. And then, they all sat back to wait for the next four days to pass.

On Friday night at about seven-forty, Heather called up the stairs to Dana. "Phone call for you!" she yelled. "It's male!"

"I wish she didn't have to announce it like I'd just won an Academy Award," Dana grumbled. Her mind wasn't on anything but the meeting the next morning, so there was clearly something lacking in her level of enthusiasm when she picked up the receiver and said, "Hello."

"Dana? It's Chris."

She hung onto the black plastic mouthpiece for a second, while feelings she didn't like at all crept to the surface. She was tempted to hang up on him, but decided that would be a really stupid move. "Chris Canby?" she asked coolly, as though he might be one of a dozen Chris's she knew.

"The one and only. Are you busy tomorrow night? I thought we might take in a movie. There's a Bogart film at the Rialto."

"Tomorrow? Oh, I'm afraid that's out of the question. This is pretty short notice," she reminded him.

"I know. Sorry about that. I've been really involved in this business project a few of the guys have been working on, and I haven't had a second free."

"What kind of project?" she asked. It was undoubtedly something horrible, like throwing old people out of their rent-controlled apartments and turning the buildings into condominiums.

"A real money-maker. But you wouldn't be interested in that," he teased.

"You're probably right," she answered promptly.

"Well, I'll let you in on it anyway. It's a cooperative effort to encourage some of the Greenleaf store-owners to hire student interns for the summer. We're trying to get Greenleaf High kids involved, too, only we want to keep the best jobs for Oakley, of course. We would have asked Canby girls to participate, but it doesn't look like any of them will be around after June."

That did it! Dana completely lost whatever control she'd managed to hang onto up till now. "Oh, you don't think so? Listen to me, Mr. Canby — don't you underestimate any of us, you hear me? Don't you dare!" With that, she slammed down the receiver so hard, she made the phone ring.

It was hard for Dana to recount her story to Shelley and Faith, because she was sputtering so much. Finally, Shelley went to the window, took a can from their pyramid of sodas, and popped it open. "Here," she said as she pressed it into Dana's shaking hand. "Drink this and calm down. He's not worth it."

Nodding vehemently, Dana consumed about half the contents of the can in a single gulp. Only then was she able to speak coherently. "You just wait, Mr. Canby," she threatened. "You and your father have another think coming!"

Saturday dawned sunny and cold, and the morning was endless. The roommates and their colleagues on the ad hoc Save Canby Hall Committee bundled up for a brisk walk to the skating pond where a few hardy souls were zipping back and forth on the ice. The picture was so serene and lovely, it tugged at all their hearts. Nobody said anything for a while, but they made a circle, almost unconsciously, and pulled it together. It was partly to block out the wind, but more, it was a gesture of faith in one another. Maybe, if they *all* pulled together, they could do something.

They tried hard to be cheerful for the rest of the morning, but even their best efforts didn't do much good. The two o'clock walk over to the headmistress' house seemed more like a funeral march than a circus parade. And the huge black limousine parked in the drive didn't make them feel the least bit better.

"Boy, I've crashed parties before, but this is something else," Cheryl muttered, twisting her long dark hair around one finger.

"Who's going to ring the doorbell?" Ellie asked, looking white and scared.

"Casey should. She has the most guts," Faith declared.

"Now just a second! I think Dana should do it. This was her idea," Casey said decisively.

"Oh, you guys . . ." Dana muttered.

"Oh, come on. Let's stop procrastinating and *do* it!" With that, Shelley marched boldly to the large oak door and rang the bell. Then she pulled her hand back sharply, as if she wanted to undo the fateful gesture. But it was too late.

In a moment, the door swung open, and Patrice Allardyce was looking down at them. She seemed very regal today, like a deposed queen, and her white silk blouse accentuated her natural pallor. "May I help you?" she asked brusquely. Then she turned back to the guest who must have been sitting in her living room. "Excuse me, please," she said with impeccable manners.

"Ms. Allardyce," Shelley began. "We're the Save Canby Hall Committee. And we saw this big car in your drive, and we thought maybe it just might be Mr. Canby. And if it is," she rushed to her conclusion, "we'd really like to speak to him. If it's okay with you, of course."

"Well, I. . . ." She frowned and once again, turned to look at her visitor. "This is highly irregular. We're in an important meeting here, girls. I'm afraid this is neither the time nor the place —"

"But we've worked so hard on our ideas, Ms. Allardyce," Faith cut in, hoping she wasn't being rude. "Besides, we didn't think it would be right for you to handle this all by yourself. We're behind you, one hundred percent."

"Please let us come in and talk to him," Dana went on. "Maybe we've come up with a few deterrents that have slipped your mind."

For once, the steely headmistress seemed to welcome their assistance. Her gray eyes were soft today, almost warm. She looked so vulnerable, so lacking in her usual control. She opened the door wide, and with an expression of gratitude that she didn't have to face Owen Canby all by herself, she let them in.

The living room was rather dark, lit only by the winter sunlight that streamed through one window. It was a comfortable room, with a flowered, chintz-covered sofa and lots of overstuffed armchairs that practically begged to be curled up in. One of the chairs was occupied by a sharp-looking, rail-thin man in his late forties with graying reddish hair. Dana could have recognized him in a crowd — he looked just like his son.

"Mr. Owen Canby, may I introduce some of the young ladies who attend our school. They are sincerely concerned about the future of Canby Hall, and, although this is not at all the kind of thing I generally encourage, I've decided to let them have their say. If this meets with your approval, of course."

Dana saw Owen Canby sneak a glance at his watch. Then he settled back more comfortably in his chair, a look of patronizing amusement on his face. "By all means, Patrice. I'm delighted to hear what the girls have to say. Naturally, this must all come as a shock to them."

"It certainly does, sir," Dana said loudly, her voice reverberating through the room. She immediately cleared her throat and started over in a softer, more conciliatory tone. "I know that you understand the meaning of school tradition, because your son attends Oakley Prep."

Mr. Canby's eyes opened a little wider. "Ah, I see someone's been doing some research. What's your name, dear?"

"Dana Morrison. And these are my roommates, Shelley Hyde and Faith Thompson." She quickly introduced the rest of the girls, and each one said a rather sullen hello to Mr. Canby. Then Dana rushed on, suddenly knowing what she had to say, and why it was so important that she be particularly eloquent. "I was a transfer student here last year, Mr. Canby, so it's not like I have the right to say that Canby Hall is in my blood. But each of us in this room has a valid reason why you shouldn't sell, and we've come to believe that we all have a right to try to make you change your mind."

Mr. Canby seemed surprised by her forceful tone. "I'm afraid, dear, that it's a little late to tell me how to run my business. I wouldn't trouble my head about these matters if I were you."

"We've already got the facts and figures," Faith told him. "We know it takes three million to run this school for a year. And yes, that's a lot of money. But we deserve it."

"Horace Canby wanted this estate to house a school, not a computer plant," Shelley continued. "He cared about education."

"Yes, young lady, in *those* long-gone days, he did. But they didn't have computers way back then. If he were alive today, he'd probably be cashing in on computers or something equally lucrative."

"Data-Tech will be the only big business in town," Faith reminded him. "They won't have any kind of network of other computer companies to deal with."

"Do you know anything about the way Data-Tech manages its product?" Mr. Canby asked.

"Well, no, but —"

"Then I suggest you not worry about how they're going to run their affairs. My dear girls, they wouldn't have wanted to buy the property if they hadn't assessed their needs at the outset."

"I think it's lousy," Casey muttered. "It stinks," she added in her typically outspoken way. There was a gasp of disapproval from Ms. Allardyce across the room, but Mr. Canby didn't seem to notice.

"Life is unfair. I totally agree with you," the man nodded.

"Why can't you just give us another year?" Joan begged. "We're trying to raise money right now, and if we do come up with a decent endowment, we'll be able to keep going all by ourselves. But you've got to give us some time."

"Just wait a few months," Ellie said. Owen Canby's answer was stony silence.

"If we could get the money, Mr. Canby," Dana ventured, "what would you say then? If we showed you that we could make this place into a financially viable business."

He threw back his head and laughed. "Now, come on. Let's be serious. A group of teen-agers could not possibly, in the wildest stretch of imagination, come up with that kind of capital."

"But if we could. . . ." Faith began.

Ms. Allardyce cut her off. She walked over to them and shook her head. "I do appreciate your coming here today, girls. Now if you'll let Mr. Canby and me finish up. . . ."

"Tell me this, sir." Dana pushed forward and walked over to face him. "What do you expect us to do at this late date if the school closes in June? How are we all going to get placed in time for next semester? Schools like this don't grow on trees, you know."

And then his face changed slightly. It was as if, before talking to the girls, he'd had a deal, juggling around pieces of paper that represented pieces of property. But now, there were human beings to contend with, and he wasn't too great at handling their mixed up feelings and emotions. Clearly, he'd never thought about the girls whose entire lives would be disrupted because of his wheeling and dealing.

"I . . . I'm sorry about all this," he said softly. "But my hands are tied. The arrangement stands."

Slowly, one by one, they walked from the room, out into the cold afternoon. The weather was nowhere near as bleak as their moods.

CHAPTER SEVEN

It was only by coincidence that Shelley and Tom ran into Mr. Sampton again. They were tooling down the Greenleaf Road on Tom's motorcycle the following Friday afternoon when they spotted a car stopped up ahead. Shelley pulled on Tom's scarf and he nodded, gradually slowing down.

The sight that greeted them was pretty funny, really. There was this old man, hopping up and down around his old Ford like an angry gremlin, kicking the tires and muttering to himself. As Shelley climbed off the cycle, she heard him say, "This dragonet, colfarnit old heap! Makes me mad just to look at your blaterast engine!" Then he noticed the young couple standing beside him. "Pardon my French, miss," he growled at her.

Shelley had missed a few vocabulary words on every test, but she was sure that was not French, nor did it bear any relation to any language spoken by man.

"What seems to be the trouble, sir?" Tom asked sympathetically.

"You think I know? If I knew, would I be standing here?" Mr. Sampton yelled.

"Let me take a look," Tom suggested. "I'm pretty good with machines." This was a very modest understatement. Tom's father swore that his son had been born with a monkey wrench in his hand. It was a mystery where he got the mechanical skills he possessed, because no one else on either side of the family could do much more than turn a light switch on and off.

"How've you been, Mr. Sampton?" Shelley asked, trying to take the man's mind off his car while Tom poked around under the hood.

"Not as good as I'd like. Not bad, though." He squinted and looked at her keenly. "I met you two before, right? At the pizza place?"

"That's right."

"You're the girl that's trying to raise all that money for your school. Cheryl, is it?"

"Shelley." Actually, she was surprised and pleased that he remembered that much.

"It seems to be your butterfly valve, sir," Tom said, looking up. "I can fix it so we can get you to the gas station. Then Mr. Bates can do the repair. Shouldn't cost a whole lot more than the new part and an hour's labor."

"And he'll soak me for it. Always does. Not a crook, though. Not him." Mr. Sampton clucked a little and raised his hands as if to say, "What can you expect from a dragonet machine like this?"

"My roommate, Faith, goes out with his son, Johnny," Shelley told him as the man got behind the wheel of his car and Tom continued to fiddle. "Maybe he'll give you a break."

"Maybe." Mr. Sampton sounded extremely disbelieving. "So, how you doing on your fund-raising?" he asked when he saw that the work would take longer than he'd wanted or expected.

"Well," Shelley sighed. "Not as great as we'd hoped. The worst part is that even if we raise the money, we're going to be dispossessed. Mr. Canby's practically made this deal with the computer company, and I guess it's all over except for some formal, legal stuff. We haven't stopped trying to raise what we need, because we're thinking that maybe we can find some temporary place to house the kids and staff for next year. But it's still going to take a lot more than we've got."

"How much you got?" he asked bluntly.

"You won't believe this. Over the past three weeks, with our preliminary letters to selected alumnae and my running around town talking to the local merchants, we've come up with five thousand dollars. I mean, we don't have it in hand, but the money's definitely promised."

Mr. Sampton nodded seriously. "And how much do you need?"

Shelley gulped. "About three million," she said in a small voice.

"Well," Mr. Sampton clucked. "Well, well, well. You try talking to this Canby fella?"

"Just last Saturday. We kind of crashed the meeting he had with our headmistress. It didn't do any good. He just laughed at us."

"Not surprised. Weak stock, all them Canbys. I remember, back in 1930 it was, my dad and Horace Canby got into a real spat over something — don't remember what it was about. But much as I can't say my father ever liked the man, he did have a certain admiration for the way he ran that school. It'd be a pity to let it go down the tubes." Then he clucked again and seemed to be thinking very hard about whatever it was that had occurred in 1930. At least, that's what Shelley figured he was thinking about.

"You can start her up now, Mr. Sampton," Tom said, coming out from under the hood and closing it. "We'll ride along with you, just to make sure you get to the gas station."

"Don't have to do that," Mr. Sampton snapped. "I'm fine."

"Just in case the colfarnit thing stops again," Tom reminded him.

"All right then," Mr. Sampton reluctantly agreed. "If you got nothing better to do, I'd be much obliged. Here she goes!" With a roar, the car was off, leaving a cloud of smoke behind it. The two kids stood looking after it, shaking their heads.

"He's weird," Tom said.

"Just doesn't like to accept help from strangers, I suppose," Shelley said. "But he was awfully nice about our problem. I didn't think he had the slightest interest in it the last time we talked to him."

"You never know about some people, do you?" Tom asked philosophically, as she climbed back on the cycle behind him. "There's always a kernel of niceness hidden inside the worst of them."

Shelley smiled and grabbed Tom around the waist. Then they zoomed off, in hot pursuit of Mr. Sampton's surprisingly speedy car.

Shelley didn't get a chance to tell Faith and Dana about the incident until the next morning, but at that point, nobody was listening. Today was the day that Yvonne Young was due on campus, and her arrival was the only thing on Faith's mind. By the time her two roommates had crawled out from under their covers, she'd already rehearsed her speech ten times in front of the bathroom mirror. She didn't want it to sound like a performance, of course, but she did want to make a good impression on the actress. Pamela had told her for sure, her mother would be there by lunchtime.

"Mr. Sampton's a great old guy, actually," Shelley was saying to Dana as they walked into the bathroom. "I just wish he were friendlier with more influential people around town."

"Yeah, me, too." Dana stopped and stared at Faith, whose lips were still moving, although her eyes were closed. "Are you praying?" Dana asked curiously.

"No, rehearsing. What time is it?"

"Eight — around there. Faith, don't wear it out. She's just a person after all. You just *talk* to her," Dana said. Then after a moment she asked, "What movie are you guys seeing with Tom and Johnny tonight?"

"Honestly, Dana, you don't sound like you're even interested in Yvonne Young," Faith complained.

"She's just unimpressed by fame and fortune," Shelley said. "And I don't blame her. Money talks, nobody walks."

"What does that mean, anyway?" Faith asked.

"I don't know. Let's have breakfast."

Pamela was already in the dining hall when they got there, sitting over a container of yogurt and a fashion magazine. She looked unlike any other Canby girl in the room. Everyone else was wearing jeans or corduroy pants with oversized sweaters — she had on a wide-shouldered coat dress in a soft mauve tweed with pink-tinted stockings and black patent pumps. She looked like she was going to a job interview. But then, Faith figured, maybe seeing her mother *was* like going to an interview. Faith glanced down at her own slacks and neat print shirt in dismay. Maybe this was inappropriate? Maybe she should dress up? But then she vetoed the idea. Being herself was her best bet.

"Let's go sit with her," Faith hissed when Dana and Shelley started across the floor toward Casey's table.

"Why should we? Hey, I'm not going to subject myself to that deliberately," Dana said vehemently. "No way."

"Please. I need moral support." Faith's dark brown eyes were pleading.

"Oh, all right," Shelley acquiesced. "But this is going to be a very brief breakfast."

"Mind if we join you?" Faith said cheerily, sliding into one of the vacant seats at the table.

Pamela scarcely looked up. "Why should I care what you do?"

"Oh, great," Dana muttered to Shelley. "We've started off on a real good foot."

"So, you haven't forgot about introducing me to your mom, have you?" Faith asked nervously.

"Dear," Pamela said patronizingly, "I never forget a promise. Don't sweat it. Unless, of course, she's not interested in meeting her public. That's a possibility, too."

They all looked up as Pamela's focus went to the window, where a long limousine had just pulled up. A head peered out from the back seat, then ducked down again.

"There she is!" Pamela exclaimed. She ran to the pegs near the door where she'd hung her camel's hair coat, and was gone.

"I better stick to her," Faith said, getting up.

Dana put a hand on her wrist and yanked her back into her seat. "Take it easy. Give her a chance to see her mother, for heaven's sake. How would you feel if you hadn't seen your mom for over six months?"

"But that's me, Dana," Faith said with a little smile. "Pamela's not human."

"Yeah, yeah, we know. Finish your eggs, nuthead." Shelley pointed at the plate. "You'll catch up with them later."

Faith had her eye peeled all morning long. She ran back to Baker after breakfast, and heard they'd been in the lounge but had just started on a tour of the campus. She took off at once, starting for the area she knew Pamela would want to show off because it looked like a movie set — the old part of the campus, Mr. Canby's original estate, which contained the farmhouse, barn and stables, the summer house beside Ms. Allardyce's home, and the old apple orchard. At last, she spotted them. They were sitting on a bench in front of the school mascot, the statue of a lioness with her cubs, which had been a gift to the school from the class of 1917, in honor of the twentieth anniversary of the school's founding.

Yvonne Young was spectacularly beautiful, with silvery blonde hair, large blue eyes, and a tall, willowy figure. Faith was impressed by how wonderful the woman looked so early in the morning on such a cold, blustery day.

Faith screwed up her courage, then casually sauntered over. "Oh, hi!" she said, as if surprised that she had run into them. "Would you mind if I joined you? I wouldn't be interrupting or anything, would I?"

Pamela's expression said that Faith was always interrupting, but she smiled grudgingly and shook her head. "Uh-uh," she said in a sweet voice. "Yvonne, you remember Faith Thompson. She's from my dorm."

"Of course," the movie star said, smiling benevolently. She removed one black-gloved hand from her lap and held it out to Faith. "How are you, dear?"

"Not very well, actually," Faith began with a dramatic sigh. "But I guess that's to be expected under the circumstances." She sighed again and sat down heavily on the bench next to Yvonne.

The actress looked puzzled. "What circumstances?"

"You haven't heard the bad news?" Faith asked. She tried to sound shocked. "I suppose Pamela hasn't told you yet because she's as upset as the rest of us are." She looked up at Yvonne imploringly. "We're all just crazy about Canby Hall," she said sincerely, patently ignoring Pamela's glare. Faith wondered if Shelley would be impressed with her acting abilities.

"Pamela, you didn't tell me there was any problem at school. What's going on?"

"Oh, there's some rumor about the school closing." Pamela tossed off the subject lightly.

"It's not a rumor anymore, Pamela. It's happening really soon — by the end of the semester, in fact. You see, Ms. Young, Canby Hall is a family business, and the old Canby who left the estate as a school never provided for an endowment. And if we don't find an endowment by June, or at least three million dollars for next year, that's it. We're kaput, finished." Faith's whole preparation, all the rehearsing she'd done, had been in vain. She'd just blown it on a few garbled, hysterical sentences.

"Oh, that's perfectly awful!" Yvonne Young clucked. "Why, I had no idea. . . ."

"I don't mean to be rude or anything," Faith continued, her heart in her stomach. "And I know it's impolite to ask —"

"Oh, Faith, don't waste my mother's time. Just ask," Pamela said in annoyance.

"But I thought you might be able to help us," Faith continued stoically. "Just because I'm always reading about people in the movie industry getting involved with worthy causes, you understand." She didn't want Yvonne Young to feel that she was leaning on her for the whole gigantic sum.

"You're perfectly right about that, dear," Ms. Young nodded. "And I'd be delighted to help my darling daughter's school." She turned and ruffled Pamela's hair, which Pamela clearly did not appreciate. "Now, you wouldn't have any way of knowing this, but back home in Hollywood, fund-raising is my thing. I can't begin to tell you the number of groups I've worked for in the past. And I love doing it. Gives you such a sense of accomplishment, you know what I mean? Like people really need you."

She stood, drawing herself up to her full height. "Consider it done. And don't worry your head about it anymore." With that, she took her daughter's arm, pulled her up beside her, and started to walk on.

Faith's mouth simply wouldn't close. When she finally realized what Yvonne Young had just promised, she saw that her benefactor was already nearly out of sight. "Wait! Wait a second! We — oh, I want to thank you! You just don't know how much this means to us all," she gasped, catching up to them at a run.

"Don't gush, Faith," Pamela said disgustedly. "You can't carry it off believably."

"It's all right, dear," Yvonne Young smiled. Then she turned to Faith. "Now you be sure to give all the information to Pamela and she'll send it on to my secretary. I'll get on it as soon as I return — and I'm sure I can get a lot of my friends involved."

"Return?" Faith suddenly had a very funny feeling.

"Yes , I'm off to Europe on the tenth. Then, let's see. . . ." The actress took a leather-and-brass appointment book from her purse. "I'll be in London for a couple of weeks seeing friends, then I'm off to Paris for some shopping, and filming with Bernardo begins in Rome on the thirtieth. We should wrap up the picture in three months or so, and then, I'm right back to Hollywood. And won't it be nice to get home after all that time?" She laughed again, a sort of carefree, isn't-life-wonderful laugh.

"But, Ms. Young, can't you do anything for us before that?" Faith said desperately. "I mean, it'll be summer by then, and everyone will have left. Most of the girls will have had to find new schools for next semester already. It's just . . . it'll be too late," she concluded lamely.

"Nonsense, dear. It's never too late," said Yvonne Young. As she and Pamela strolled off arm in arm, she called over her shoulder, "It'll be my pleasure to get you girls an endowment. And what a nice little blurb I'll get in the paper."

As Faith watched them go, she had to laugh a little. When you dealt with movie stars, you had to be prepared for the unbelievable. Well, she thought, meandering slowly back to the dorm, she'd done what she'd set out to do — she had a promise of tons of money. Of course, it wouldn't help save Canby Hall the least little bit.

CHAPTER EIGHT

I wish you'd change your mind." Faith looked at Dana pleadingly.

"It's just a movie — it's not like we've got these heavy dates you'd be horning in on. You know Tom and Johnny think of you as part of our group, anyhow," Shelley added.

"That sounds real great, Shel," Dana sighed. "Just part of the group, just a piece of the wallpaper." She made a face and went back to doing her nails, which today, were about to be painted passion pink.

"She didn't mean that. It's just stupid, your not going out on Saturday nights. And whether you're with a guy or not shouldn't make any difference," Faith pointed out. "We just like to have you with us."

Dana smiled grudgingly. "I know. I didn't mean to bite your heads off. But honest, I'd rather stay in tonight. I've got a great novel that's been begging me to read it, and besides, I want to go over our lists of donors and alumnae. You guys have fun, okay?"

Her roommates looked at her, and then at one another. Shelley was about to make one more protest when Heather knocked on the door and announced that the boys had arrived and were waiting downstairs in the lounge.

"Okay, all right. This week, we'll go without you," Faith sighed, as she signed out on the form attached to their door and then handed the pencil to Shelley. "But next week —"

"Next week I may have a date with an Italian count, or a British millionaire, or something equally exciting. Now, get out of here!" Dana yelled, pushing them out the door and closing it. They were neat, really, but sometimes, she just needed to be alone.

It was okay not having a boyfriend around right at this point in her life. When she broke up with Bret, months ago, she didn't think she could bear it. Everything — the movies, the pizza parlor, the wooded paths where they used to go for romantic walks — it all reminded her of him. As for Randy, she liked him a lot, but they were so different that the romantic side of their relationship was almost an afterthought. He would always be her friend, but she doubted that it could go further than that.

Now with Randy in Kentucky, she was on her own. And she was getting used to it. If she fell in love again, the guy would have to be pretty special. Just a couple of months earlier, she thought she'd found that guy in Peter Marks, a handsome film technician who'd been with the film company that shot a movie at Canby Hall. But he had proved himself to be about as fickle as they come. Dana wasn't hurt or angry anymore, though. She even had to smile to herself, remembering the fun they'd had together.

She blew on her nails, pronounced them dry, and then gathered up her novel and clipboard full of papers to go sit in the lounge. It was cozy down there, and she loved curling up in one of the big antique chairs and trying to become part of the Canby Hall that once had been, many, many decades ago.

There were two freshmen playing cards quietly, and a couple of sophomores she didn't know very well. That was it.

Guess I'm the only junior with sense enough to stay home on a freezing Saturday night, she consoled herself. The hum of some classical music on the radio station was the only sound in the room, and Dana was pleased to see that her favorite chair was vacant. She was just about to settle in when one of the phones in the bank that lined the lounge started to ring.

"I'm up, I'll get it," she told everyone. She picked up on the fourth ring. "Hi, Baker House," she said.

"Could I please speak to . . . Dana, is that you?" the voice on the other end asked.

"Yes, who's this?" She knew, but she didn't want to let on.

"Chris Canby, who else? Listen, I'm really sorry about our last phone call. I didn't mean to get you all riled up."

"Chris, I don't get riled up. I get mad." She felt very sure of herself tonight.

"Well, I want to make it up to you. I want to make you *not* mad at me — how's that sound?"

She smirked at the phone, trying to imagine what was coming. "Yes?" she prompted.

"I know you hate to get asked out on short notice, but this is my father's fault — not mine. He wants me to come over for brunch tomorrow — just called me this second. And I'm inviting you."

Dana was silent for a moment. Then she said, "Why do you want me to come?"

"Hey, remember, I told you I wanted to get to know you. I'd really like to see you, Dana. And to put an end to this adversarial relationship that has somehow managed to spring up between us. Let's bury the hatchet under some eggs Benedict tomorrow. Pick you up at eleven, how's that?"

Dana's mind worked quickly. Lunch with Owen Canby would mean another opportunity to convince him. He'd be a prisoner in his own home, forced to listen to her arguments. And he was probably a very proper Bostonian — he wouldn't throw out one of his son's guests or tell her to shut up. Then, there was something else. She kind of admired Chris, for his persistence if for no other reason.

"Okay, I'll go. What do I wear?"

"Nothing special. Your gorgeous face will do. And maybe some jeans and a sweater."

Dana found herself blushing. With a promise to be waiting in front of Baker promptly at eleven o'clock, she said good-night and hung up. There was a lot to be said for a guy who disagreed with all your principles but would defend to the death your right to have them.

Shelley and Faith applauded Dana's decision to go. "At least you get a second shot at him," Faith declared.

"Try for right between the eyes," Shelley suggested. "He deserves it, the creep."

"Why, Shel, I don't think I've ever heard you use that word," Dana laughed.

Shelley made a fist and shook it. "He who threatens my school, threatens me. I'll say worse than that before this is over. Do your worst, Dana."

It took a little over an hour to get from Greenleaf to Beacon Hill in Boston, which gave Dana and Chris a chance to get to know one another. He wasn't all stock portfolios and real estate deals, although he did drive a brand new Fiat Spider. Dana's parents had always taught her that money was nice to have, but it wasn't everything, and she had a healthy respect for people who knew how to have a great time on very little. On the other hand, there was probably something to be said for terribly rich people who didn't flaunt it. And Chris seemed to be one of these. They discussed jogging and marathoning for about half an hour, and he never once mentioned the top-of-the-line running shoes Dana had seen him wearing that day they met.

His parents, however, were not as reticent about showing off their assets. As they pulled into the drive in front of the Canby home, Dana had to gasp. The house was a mansion, plain and simple. Two large white stone lions guarded the entranceway to a veranda paved in green marble. It was breathtaking.

"Is it okay if we walk on this?" Dana whispered as Chris showed her up the steps to the gigantic doors with gleaming brass knockers.

"Yeah, as long as you tiptoe. Don't want to wear it out in the next millenium. Oh, hi, Travers — how's things?" Chris asked the elegantly uniformed butler who answered the door.

"Your mother is in the drawing room, sir," said the poker-faced, plump man who showed them inside. A maid quickly relieved Dana of her parka, which made her feel really strange. They walked down a long corridor lined with what must have been original oil paintings, and then into the sun-filled drawing room at the very end of the hall.

At first, all Dana could see was plants.

There were tall palms and short, stocky orange trees, various smaller plants, and plenty of ferns hanging from the ceiling. Then, amid the greenery, she spotted a very small woman with prematurely white hair sitting on a velvet couch, her hands folded in her lap. "Hello, Chris dear," she said.

"Hi, Mom. How are you? Mom, this is my friend, Dana Morrison."

"I'm pleased to meet you, dear." Mrs. Canby presented one rather limp hand to Dana for her to shake. She couldn't help but notice that the woman's manner was as humble and withdrawn as her husband's was arrogant and self-assured. This was *not* a person who expressed her own feelings when they ran against the tide, Dana surmised.

"It's great to be here. You have a lovely home," Dana said, remembering her manners.

Mrs. Canby unfolded her hands, and one of them strayed nervously to an imaginary stray hair on her forehead. "I can't imagine what's keeping your father, Chris. He just isn't aware of the time these days," she apologized to Dana.

"Hey, I have that problem all the time," Dana smiled.

"But you don't have a beeper that rings you every hour on the hour," Chris pointed out. "I sometimes wonder if he could survive without his beeper. It would be awful, you know. A scion of the community, a well-to-do businessman falling completely apart for the lack of his beeper."

Dana bit the insides of her cheeks to keep herself from laughing. The amazing thing was that Chris hadn't said it in a sarcastic way at all, but just as though it were a particularly interesting scientific problem.

"Oh, here he is! Dear, Chris has brought us a little friend."

Little friend! Dana felt herself growing hot. She was taller than most girls, and she was nearly a grown woman — sixteen years old! What was the matter with Mrs. Canby, anyway?

"Son, good to see you." Mr. Canby strode across the room to shake Chris's hand, and Dana noticed that steely look in his eyes. Today, he was casually dressed in a soft, wine-colored cashmere sweater and black slacks. "And whom have we here?" As he turned to her, his face hardened subtly, almost imperceptibly. Only Dana noticed it. "I think, if I'm not mistaken, that we've met before."

"That's right, sir," Dana said politely, extending her hand. "At Ms. Allardyce's last Saturday."

"What?" Chris gave her a puzzled look. "How come you didn't say anything?"

Dana shrugged innocently. "It must have slipped my mind."

Mrs. Canby, who looked exceedingly bored by this whole interchange, got up, smoothing her perfect ultrasuede skirt, and walked over to open the drawing-room doors that led to an enclosed dining alcove, a breathtaking solarium with a domed glass roof and paneled glass walls. Dana felt like she herself was a hothouse plant as she stepped inside after her hostess.

"Why don't we all sit down?" Mrs. Canby asked as she rang a small brass bell. A uniformed waitress appeared immediately from behind a tree, as though she'd been there all the time, just waiting for her cue.

Dana started for the chair nearest her and had her hand on the back of it when she felt it practically yanked from her.

"Allow me," Chris said with a twinkle in his eye as he pulled it out for her. She could tell by the unnecessary flourish he made as he pulled it out that this was for his parents' benefit, not hers.

"We'll have the first course, now, Marie," Mrs. Canby murmured to the maid, who vanished as soundlessly as she had come.

"I wasn't aware you were acquainted with my son," Owen Canby said pleasantly to Dana. "Although I should have guessed. You knew he went to Oakley, didn't you?"

"Mmm," Dana nodded, watching the parade of dishes that were entering the room on the arms of not one but five serving people. "We met while jogging one day, actually."

"Dana's thinking of training for a marathon, Dad," Chris said. "Now that takes stamina. And courage."

"Yes, it does. But I'm not surprised. I noticed the other day that you certainly had the courage of your convictions. I like that. Have you ever tried kippered herring, Miss Morrison?" Mr. Canby, having filled his plate, sat back to watch Dana's slight discomfort as she glanced at the serving platters before her. There were these long, brown fish with beady eyes lying in rows, with parsley between them. They certainly didn't look like anything anyone in her right mind would eat. But if Mr. Canby could take it, so could she.

"I haven't had them in ages," she said, taking the smallest. Then she reached over to the next platter and took a gigantic slice of cranshaw melon with a wedge of lime. As an afterthought, she took some asparagus with hollandaise sauce from the third platter and placed it on her bread-and-butter plate. She knew at once by the reaction that she'd made a fatal error in judgment.

A disapproving waitress immediately removed the plate and allowed her helper to reposition the asparagus on its proper-sized receptacle. Then she took another plate from her tray, put a roll and a curl of butter on it and positioned it to the right and just above Dana's lace placemat.

Whew! she thought. It was like a diagram for a foolproof military campaign. Every bush and model soldier had to be meticulously in order, or the war couldn't go on.

"Chris, dear, your fish fork," his mother

reminded him when Chris began attacking his kipper with the perfectly ordinary fork to the left of his plate.

Dana looked over and realized that Chris had made a mistake for her benefit. She had had no idea what those skinny little forks with only three tines were for, and she never would have picked one up if it hadn't been for Chris. With a look of determination that she hoped would pass for enjoyment, she dug in.

"The deal's going through as planned," Mr. Canby said as he tore apart his fish and managed to remove about a hundred infinitesimal bones before beginning to eat. "Data-Tech is signing the contracts at the end of the month, and from there on, it's clear sailing."

"Great, Dad. Looks like you've handled this one with your usual aplomb." This time, Chris didn't look at Dana. He knew this was the one subject they couldn't make private jokes about.

"Do you think, Mr. Canby," Dana said, giving up on the fish and going on to the melon, "that it might be possible to make three parties happy instead of just two? I mean, suppose our committee does earn the kind of money we mentioned last week. I know you have your obligations to these computer people, but what about settling Canby Hall in some temporary place, like — oh, I don't know, an old armory, or a fire station. We could probably take some classes at Oakley or Greenleaf High with our own teachers, and even though the living accommodations wouldn't be so hot, we'd still have our school. What do you think about that?"

Mr. Canby looked at the ceiling, then at his son as if to say, "You have your nerve bringing this troublemaker into our hallowed home." But Dana had been right about his sense of propriety. He wouldn't let on that he was annoyed.

"I don't see how it's conceivable at this late date. Is there some kind of facility like this armory or fire station currently available?"

"Well, I don't know that, but I thought maybe you could —"

Chris cut her off with a raised fish fork. "Dana, my father said no. No is no."

There was silence in the room as one of the maids poured coffee and passed the elaborate silver creamer and sugar bowl. Mrs. Canby cleared her throat. Chris tore off a piece of roll. Mr. Canby continued to eat steadily and efficiently. Dana wanted to get right up and walk out.

But then, just as things were getting particularly deadly, Chris said, "Dad, you know that old abandoned lumber mill on the creek, sort of near Melrose?"

Dana's heart skipped about twenty beats. It was in that very mill that Shelley'd been held captive by kidnappers last year when they mistook her for Casey.

"I don't know the particular mill you have

in mind, son. There are so many of them up that way."

"I was just thinking. That contractor you always use, Pete Rachinello — he's fast and cheap. He might be able to convert a mill into a dorm and some classrooms over the summer. I mean, it would mostly be the girls' money — all these millions they're raising." He winked at Dana.

She was so excited she could hardly speak. "Even if you couldn't get the classrooms done," she said, "you could charter some kind of bus service for us and ship us over to Oakley for classes. The Canby Hall teachers could just use whatever classrooms weren't occupied. It's a wonderful idea! Oh, Chris, you're a genius!" She wanted to get up and hug him.

But then, just as the eggs Benedict were served, Mr. Canby tabled the discussion. "I really think we're boring your mother, son. What say we all talk about something else? Shall we?" he added pointedly.

Dana ate her eggs in silence, feeling her teeth grind with every bite. Why should Owen Canby want to lift a finger to help them, after all? Why should he bother concerning himself with contractors and lumber mills and chartered buses? He'd made his deal, he nearly had his money — and that was all that mattered to him. She hated the man. The intensity of her feelings astounded her.

On the way home later that afternoon, Chris

took one hand off the steering wheel and covered hers as it lay on the leather seat cover. "Sorry, Dana," he sighed as they zipped along the highway. "I thought one of us would offer him an alternative he'd find mildly palatable. But I guess he doesn't have his mind on charity cases right now. And that's all the defunct Canby Hall is to him."

"It's okay," she lied. "You tried."

"I haven't given up. You better not, either."

She looked over at him, puzzled. "I don't get it. You told me you agreed with your father, that this was the right business decision. Yet now you're on our side. What's your *real* opinion?" She hated people who waffled on both sides of an issue.

Chris kept his eyes on the road and shrugged. "The sale of the property is good business — I haven't turned around on that. But I also think your school is an important community asset. So I want to help. I'm going to keep working on him, Dana. You may have lost Canby Hall for good, but there's no reason you should lose all your friends and the kind of education you were getting. Maybe we'll think of something by the end of June. That's months away."

"Sure," she nodded. But she wasn't so sure anymore. She had been the firebrand, the one who laughed in the face of doom and destruction. Now, there was nothing to laugh at, and lots to cry about. When Chris pulled to a stop in front of Baker House thirty minutes later, she was almost resigned. She'd return to New York, she'd live with her mother and Maggie, and next year, when her father and Eve and their new baby got back to the city, she'd spend a lot of time with them. As a matter of fact, this would be the perfect summer to take them up on their invitation and vacation with them in Hawaii. Maybe she'd call her dad tomorrow.

"Dana, I really like you — you know that?" she heard Chris say beside her. "We're different as two people can be, but somehow, that doesn't matter." Then, he kissed her softly. It didn't make her forget anything, but it was very, very nice.

CHAPTER NINE

The next flier that came around to the dorms was the worst one the girls had ever received from the hand of Ms. Allardyce.

"Please be informed that several members of Mr. Owen Canby's staff and the representatives of the Data-Tech company will be on campus this coming Saturday to take inventory. As I will be out of town for the week on business and unable to supervise, I am requesting that you cooperate with your teachers and houseparents completely on this matter. Thank you. Patrice Allardyce."

"Even her signature looks shaky," Casey sighed, crumpling up her flier into the tightest ball possible. "I think she's about to crack."

"You and your amateur psychologizing," Shelley grinned. The girls were all sitting around the lounge, waiting out the hailstorm that spattered the windows and shook the bare tree limbs. "Where do you think she's going on business?"

"Looking for another job at another school, I bet," Joan Barr declared angrily.

"You're totally wrong about that," Dana said, getting up and beginning to pace. "She's not deserting us."

"But what's she going to do now, Dana?" Faith asked, her pencil going over and over the doodle she'd drawn on the pad in front of her. "If we don't have a place to relocate, and we don't have Mr. Canby's support, it's curtains for us. And for her, too."

They were interrupted by the sounds of loud arguing in the hallway. Cheryl tiptoed to the partly open lounge door and peeked through. "It's Michael and Alison," she whispered.

"Lover's quarrel?" asked Casey cynically. Dana gave her a dirty look. But then the door opened all the way and the couple walked into the room, so they didn't have to guess.

"You guys are not going to believe this," Alison announced, her reddish-brown hair flying everywhere, "but let me try it on for size. In Ms. Allardyce's absence next week, Michael and I have been appointed temporary heads of the school. Chief monitors of all the headaches."

"Yay! Terrific! Long live the king and queen!" Various girls popped up from their positions on the floor to do little improvised dances of happiness. Everyone was thinking the same thought — it could have been the Druyans in Addison House, who were notoriously strict.

"So you've got to behave. And pass the word along to everyone in the other houses that *they* have to behave," Michael warned. "Alison and I are not tolerating any monkey business, got it?" The wink at the end of his sentence belied his serious tone.

"What's this inventory stuff about?" demanded Dana, waving the flier, her mind still on the problem at hand. "Do they get all our desks and lockers and lab equipment and everything?"

"Guess that was part of Mr. Canby's arrangement," Michael nodded. "The buyer in a big deal like this is supposed to know the entire worth of his property. I suppose they can sell what they don't need or auction it off."

"Not the Round Table! They can't get rid of the Round Table," Shelley wailed dramatically. Just the thought of scrapping that beautiful piece of wood in the library that had all those generations of Thespians' initials carved into it tore at her soul.

"Shelley, it's out with the old and in with the new. I hate it just as much as you do, but that's the way it's gotta be. Who's started on their applications for new schools?" Alison asked briskly. "The guidance counselor here," she jerked her head at Michael, "is open for business, and I suggest you all make private appointments with him to discuss your future plans."

"I can't believe she just said that," Faith murmured under her breath.

"Alison, you mean . . . you think it's over?" Shelley asked pitifully. "With all the fund-raising we've been doing, and everything, you're just saying go get into some other schools? That's sheer insanity. Didn't mean to be rude," she added, when Alison sucked in her cheeks.

"That's okay, sweetie. I know how you feel. But Michael and I have just been discussing it" — again, that look! — "and my thought is that we all have to buckle down and get practical. I don't want anybody left out in the cold when this is all over. Now, look," she went on to the assembled long faces, "I'm not saying you should stop your efforts to get us cash or find us a new place. I just think you should also prepare for the worst. Michael disagrees," she added.

"You bet I do," he said emphatically. He plopped himself down on the floor between Casey and Joan. "Once you've put in an application somewhere else, you've started thinking about going to that place. And whether you get in or not, your concentration is divided. How can you be loyal to Canby Hall and really work for its survival when you're hoping and praying that Sanford Academy will take you?"

Casey held her nose. "Who'd want to go to Sanford Academy? Yuk!"

"That was just an example, silly," Faith said. "I see your point, Michael. But then, how *do* you know when to give up? When to divide your loyalty?"

Michael looked at the ceiling for an answer. When none came, he shrugged. "You feel it in your bones. My bones say, it's not time yet."

"Well, my stomach says, 'Feed me, or else!' How about it, Mr. Frank? Shall we adjourn to the faculty dining room?" Alison suggested. "I'm sure these girls have a lot to discuss."

He pulled himself up and glanced around at the assembled crew. " 'To everything there is a season,' " he quoted, " 'a time to be born and a time to die, a time to sow and a time to reap,' a time to ditch your school and a time to hang on by your fingernails. Even when they're chewed to the quick. Ecclesiastes," he intoned with a little smirk on his face. And then he took Alison's arm and marched her out the door.

"Is that really in the Bible?" Eileen Davis asked incredulously. "Wow!"

No one bothered to answer her.

It was probably about midnight when Casey sat up in bed, her eyes shining. "Hey!" she said aloud. She slipped out of bed, jumped into her robe and slippers and padded down the corridor to Room 407. Without knocking, she let herself in. "Guys? Anybody up?"

"Umm?" Faith murmured sleepily.

"I just thought of something really important," Casey said, going from mattress to mattress, trying to rouse them.

"I'm asleep," Shelley groaned.

"In the morning," Dana sighed, turning over.

"Won't wait till then. Aw, c'mon, you three. Look alive." Casey reached over and turned on the lamp that sat on the antique marble-topped table between the beds.

"Turn it off!" Faith croaked. She reached out for the switch, but Casey was wide awake and therefore at an advantage.

"No, you don't! Next step is a glass of cold water in each face in the room. The alternative is listening to me. What's the verdict?"

Slowly, each girl pulled herself from the warmth of the covers and sat huddled against a pillow, glaring at Casey.

"This better be good," Dana warned.

"Okay, I thought of something. We can foil Mr. Canby — at least temporarily," Casey looked at each of them in turn. "Now, how do they know, when they march in here on Saturday, what's theirs and what's ours? How do they know, for instance, that this marble-topped table is legally yours?"

"Because Ms. Allardyce must have a list somewhere of the school's inventory. They just want to make sure no one stole a bed or a microscope, Case — they won't be counting

antique tables," Faith explained patiently.
"Except the ones in the Baker House lounge.
That stuff goes with the assets."

"Exactly what I meant!" Casey said triumphantly.

"But everything in the lounge will be on
the list, Casey," Shelley said patiently, as if
explaining to a particularly slow child.

"Not if we move the lounge furniture, or
even switch it for the stuff in Charles House.
That'd get 'em going!" she cackled. "They
wouldn't know whose, was what's, was where."

The three roommates scowled at Casey.
"That's your brilliant scheme? Moving things
around? Casey, that sounds like a twelve-year-
old's idea of a practical joke. Do you realize
how long it would slow them down? And
besides," Faith added grumpily, *"we'd* be the
ones who'd have to move everything back
again. Go to sleep, will you?"

"All right, okay," Casey conceded. "That
was a stinker. I was just trying it out to whet
your appetites. But I have another idea, and
you're going to love it. If you don't, I will
personally brain every one of you. The only
problem with it is that every girl in the school
has to go along with it. Now, here's what we're
really going to do on Saturday. . . ."

As Dana, Faith, and Shelley listened to
Casey's scheme, they all sat up a little
straighter in bed. When she was finished, she
had three slightly dubious but very interested
helpers. At one a.m., they agreed to take no-

tices around personally to every Canby Hall student first thing in the morning.

"You really think this is going to do any good?" Shelley asked one final time before Casey said good-night.

"Well, it can't do any harm. And it will give us the kind of public forum we need for our fund-raising. Once we're through with those guys, there won't be a soul in Greenleaf who isn't aware of our plight," Casey finished forcefully. As she closed the door to their room, she added, "That's the first time in my life I've ever said 'plight.' "

The brief memo was drafted before breakfast, and by first period, Dana had already run off two-hundred-fifty copies on the library's mimeograph machine. At lunchtime, the roommates and Casey canvassed the dining hall, nabbing every girl who would listen. They'd given out a hundred memos by dinner, where they got rid of a few dozen more. After Study Hours, they hit the lounges of the other two houses, and then got the last stragglers in Baker just before lights-out.

They were exhausted at the end of the day, having talked themselves silly. The plan, however, had caught fire. The most amazing convert was Pamela Young, of all people. Since coming to Canby Hall, she'd hardly joined in on any extracurriculars, seeming to take the attitude that she was above it all. But somehow, this idea seemed to appeal to her. Or maybe the thought of trying to get into another school was more than she could cope with.

"We've done it," Casey declared as they sat around Room 407 in the dark.

"I'm not exactly sure what we've done," Faith said. "But I'll tell you one thing. Those inventory guys are going to get the shock of their lives on Saturday morning."

Shelley went to the windowsill and took down a few cans of Tab from their rapidly diminishing pyramid. "This deserves a toast," she smiled, passing out the drinks.

The sound of four pop-tops snapping resounded in the room with all the flourish of champagne corks going off.

CHAPTER TEN

It was fair and cold on Saturday, without the trace of a cloud in the sky. Everyone was ready and had been for days. Shelley, Joan, and several others of the Thespians had raided the prop closet of the theater and come up with three lengths of chains from an old production of *A Christmas Carol*. They were a little rusty, but they'd do. Every girl who owned a bike on campus was bringing her lock, and most of those had pretty good steel cables attached to them. The girls who didn't have anything were just going to bring several lengths of belts and position themselves in inconspicuous places.

Everyone had some sort of poster or placard. Some were hand-lettered signs, stating demands in a direct, no-nonsense manner. A SCHOOL IS A SCHOOL! and GIVE CANBY HALL BACK TO THE STUDENTS! were two of the most obvious. Some were blow-ups of Faith's gorgeous photographs of the campus, with captions under them. Faith's own favorite, and the one she carried proudly, was her shot of the dorms as seen hazily through the park with the wishing pool in the foreground. She'd taken the photograph on a blustery, gray day, and the focus of the picture was an incorporeal wisp of fog floating up from the water that did, in fact, look as much like a ghost as anything else. The caption to the poster read, "Horace Canby (1865–1936) Opposes Sale of Canby Hall. Turn back now before it's too late!"

"That oughta scare the pants off 'em," Casey had declared when she saw the poster.

Dana and Casey had handed out the place assignments. At least fifteen girls would be needed per house — fifty at the library, fifty at the science building, and fifty at the main building. That left only fifty or so extra bodies for the sports complex, infirmary, and grounds department. They didn't bother covering the old parts of the campus — the summer house, chapel, carriage house, and farmhouse didn't contain any crucial property.

The only remaining question early Saturday morning was whether to tell Michael and Alison. Dana and Shelley were strongly in favor, Faith and Casey opposed, and the other girls who made up the core of the Save Canby Hall Committee — Cheryl, Joan, Ginny, and Ellie — were pretty equally split. At the last minute, just before the inventory-takers were due to arrive, they decided to flip a coin.

"Heads, we tell!" Dana said triumphantly, leading the way upstairs to Alison's apartment in Baker's penthouse. "C'mon, we don't have much time."

"I think this is real dumb," Casey said. "She's got to try to stop us. Just remember, Miss Goody-Goody, we're informing her of our intentions — not asking permission."

"I understand that, Casey," Dana said patiently as she knocked on the door. A loud meow came back in response.

"Good morning," Alison smiled, gathering Doby, her calico cat, into her arms before he could escape out the door.

"Alison," Faith said grimly, "we have some news for you. There's nothing you can do about it even if you want to, because the plan's been set in motion, but we did feel it only fair to warn you."

Alison shook her head, as though she couldn't quite believe what she'd just heard. "What's going on?"

"We're staging a sit-in," Casey informed her. "Every building's going to be barricaded so the men can't get through to take their inventory. We're not going to use force, of course — it's passive resistance all the way — but we don't intend to let them pass. That's all we have to say." She turned on her heel and stomped downstairs, but Shelley and Dana felt compelled to add something. The other girls kind of straggled down behind Casey.

"This is the only way we can get our cause known, Alison," Shelley explained. "People in this town may not think we're serious about keeping Canby Hall running. Well, this will show them that we're going to fight — to the death."

"Not fight," Dana corrected her. "This is just our way of stating our rights. I know this puts you in an awfully tough position, Alison, as acting headmistress and all, but we *have* to do it. Do you understand? The press coverage we're sure to get may be enough to buy us some time — maybe even enough time to collect all the money from the big donors, like Pamela's mother. We're really sorry if this gets you into trouble."

Before Alison could protest, Dana took Shelley's arm and dragged her down the stairs, not wanting to hear the housemother's arguments. And Alison, to her credit, didn't bother going after them. First, she buzzed Michael on the interoffice phone. Then, she ransacked her apartment for the number in Boston that Ms. Allardyce had given her.

Dana and Shelley were out the door as soon as they had their coats and hats on, running to join the others at their battle stations. Everyone had been instructed to wear layers of clothing, including two pairs of socks under boots, hats and mufflers, and tights under their jeans or pants. They'd also stocked up on cookies, chips, and snacks from the machines, just in case it turned out to be a very long haul. No thermoses of coffee, though. Once they got into formation, they wouldn't be able to get out, so they'd all decided the best and most comfortable course of action was not to drink anything all morning.

"Are we okay?" asked Nancy Palmer when Faith and Casey were within shouting distance of Main Building. There were girls everywhere, on the stairs, tucked into the doorway, spilling around the entrance porch. The bike cables went around their waists and the locks attached them to the next girl in line. The two girls on each end had hooked onto the banisters or porch railings.

"Wonderful!" Casey said. "Looks like we're prisoners on a chain gang. Positively gruesome!" She cackled with glee as Dana and Shelley caught up. "Come on, room for two more!"

"I want to check the other buildings — make sure they have everything they need," Dana told her. "Be right back. You're terrific, girls!" she shouted to the assembled troops.

"Right on!" someone yelled.

"We'll never give up!"

"We'll show those guys who's boss."

The spirit, the team feeling, was palpable in the air. Everyone — freshmen, sophomores, juniors, and seniors — was united in this vital cause, and everyone was determined to stick it out, no matter what it cost them. Dana,

Faith, and Shelley had warned them that this incident would undoubtedly go on all their records. "But, of course, if the whole school does it," Cheryl had pointed out sensibly, "they can't pinpoint the troublemakers."

Dana ran from building to building, checking to make sure that everyone was securely locked in, their posters at the ready. "Remember," she told the girls at the science building, where Joan Barr was in charge, "don't unlock yourselves, no matter what they promise. The point is to wait until the media gets here. Even if we run the guys off campus, they could come back ten minutes later, so stay at your post until Casey, Faith, or I come get you. And good luck!"

She checked the three dorms, then quickly got over to the library. When she saw Michael coming across the path, walking straight toward her, she started to run. She had to get back to Main Building and get hooked up to the others before he caught her.

But Michael had been her jogging partner often enough that past fall to know where her weak spots were. He could outrun her if he tried, and so he did. "Hey, Dana," he called as he ran, "cut it out. I'm too old for this."

Reluctantly, she came to a standstill. They were both puffing hard. "Don't try to talk me out of it."

"All right, I won't. But I have to tell you it's not going to get you anywhere. This is not

Michael Frank, guidance counselor, speaking, it's a guy who used to sit in and protest and march for every cause that came along when he was in high school and college. Believe me, I'm experienced."

"So?" she asked somewhat sullenly, glancing at her watch.

"So you win for a few hours. You feel righteous and together and oh, so indignant. You're the good guys; they're the baddies. But look at it this way — they have the power, ultimately, and they'll be back with chainclippers. I just hope the publicity you want is worth it. And to show you what a guy I am," he added, his face a completely blank mask, "I intend to put through some anonymous calls to the Greenleaf *Chronicle* and the Boston *Globe* and *Herald* myself. Hey," he said when she looked at him with shining, thankful eyes. "I'm not helping you. I just want to get this thing over with before Ms. Allardyce storms back onto campus and blames me."

"Thanks, Michael," Dana said, reaching out briefly to touch his hand. "You're a pal." Then she was running again, because she heard the far-distant sounds of several cars in the distance. The last thing she saw as she put her bicycle chain around her waist and joined it to Casey's and Ellie's was Michael's departing back, on his way to his place in the East Faculty houses. She didn't tell anyone about their conversation.

"Okay, it's about to begin," Casey informed the throng behind her. "What's the good word?"

"We're going to win!" someone yelled.

"We're here to stay!" called a few more voices.

Dana raised a hand to quiet them. "Don't wear yourselves out, and don't get all hoarse before they get here. Remember, there's a purpose to this. Let's not waste it."

Casey, who'd been trying to fan some flame into the fires on this cold morning, gave her a dirty look, but shrugged as she conceded that the less energy they spent before the men arrived, the more they'd have for the event itself.

They didn't have long to wait. The first car, a blue Mercedes, pulled around in front of Main Building two minutes later, followed by two Pontiacs, and a van marked "Data-Tech."

"This is it," Faith whispered to Shelley under her breath. She gave her hand a squeeze, and in turn, Shelley passed it on to Casey who passed it on to Dana. "Keep your fingers crossed."

"I can't," Casey complained. "They're frozen already."

Ten men and one woman, all with clip-boards except for Owen Canby who'd just appeared from the back of the Mercedes, started for the building with very puzzled expressions on their faces. Then, as they got closer, the quizzical looks turned to angry ones.

Mr. Canby pushed his way through the group and stood before the front line of girls, tapping one gloved hand against the opposite wrist in annoyance. "Is this some kind of joke?"

There was silence for a moment, and then Casey said, "It's no joke. You can't get through. And it's no good trying the other buildings on campus, either. They're all barricaded. We're protesting the inventory, Mr. Canby, just as we're protesting the sale of our school."

His face turned red, then white, as he looked at the assembled faces and read some of the placards. His gaze stopped on Dana. "You! I should have known. Why, you little. . . . I offer you the hospitality of my home and you don't even have the decency to appreciate it. Kids!" he grunted, turning to the man who must have been his private secretary. "Get Ms. Allardyce over here right away."

"She's not here, sir," Dana said politely. "She's out of town on business. And I tried to talk to you when I came to your home. I tried to prevent all this. You wouldn't listen, though. You simply dismissed me as though I were a silly child. Well, I'm not — none of us are. We have rights and we intend to make them known to the community."

Where were the reporters? This was awful.

"You have rights! You don't comprehend the first thing about legal matters, young ladies," said one of the men who'd gotten out of the Data-Tech van. "And before you get yourselves in a great deal of hot water, why don't you all reconsider and let us pass. I don't think you want the kind of trouble we can make, so let's cooperate, shall we?" He took a step toward them, but nobody moved.

"This is absurd," the woman in the group said. "Why are we standing around arguing with a bunch of kids? There must be someone in charge. I'm going to find whoever it is." With that, she stalked off, her high heels clicking on the brick path.

"Girls," Mr. Canby stated, trying to control his anger and sound rational and reasonable, "you all know that the school is going to be sold. And no matter how much money you raise or how long you chain yourselves to the buildings, you aren't going to influence the deal one way or another. The sooner you all realize that you're powerless to change anything, the better."

"But the sale isn't final yet, is it?" Faith asked hesitantly.

"Well, yes, for all intents and purposes. The papers will be signed —"

"*Will* be signed," Faith repeated. "My point exactly. Until such time as all the formalities are over with, you can't just barge in here and treat us like we don't belong. At the present moment, Canby Hall is still ours."

"She's absolutely right!" several voices chimed in.

"Come back when you've got a contract!" someone else called.

Everyone waved their posters in the air, and the group suddenly seemed to mobilize behind Faith, all cheering her on. They were still making a racket when a second group of cars and vans pulled up.

"Look, Dana! A camera crew!" Casey chortled in glee as the WBZ news team piled out with their equipment. Reporters, their notebooks and microphones preceding them into the fray, charged the group of inventory-takers and pushed them aside, except for one particularly aggressive woman who recognized Owen Canby and started grilling him for information.

"Why are you girls chained to the buildings?" asked a reporter.

"We're protesting the sale of Canby Hall. We want it stopped, right away!" Ellie told him.

"Mr. Canby, what do you have to say in response?"

"I'm only doing what I have to do. . . ."

The interview went on for a good fifteen minutes. Casey, Dana, and Faith answered most of the questions, and the rest of the girls kept their posters high enough for the camera-men to get good shots. By the time the reporters were finished and wrapping up the story, most of the Data-Tech people had fled inside their van, and Mr. Canby's associates were barricaded in their cars. The woman who had gone off earlier in search of somebody in charge returned with Alison and Michael, and while she whispered in Mr. Canby's ear, the acting heads of the school also got questioned. Alison looked distraught; Michael looked barely tolerant.

"And what do you intend to do about your inventory, Mr. Canby?" the short, pushy reporter hounded him.

"I'm going to get it a little later today, as a matter of fact." Mr. Canby had sounded unbelievably cool and collected throughout the whole ordeal. "One of my people has just informed me that she's been on the phone with the Greenleaf sheriff, and he's on his way over with several squad cars. We're going to put a stop to this foolishness at once."

"The sheriff!" Eileen Davis squealed.

"Are you going to get us arrested?" Casey demanded.

"I believe that's what they call it when they haul you off to jail for some wrongdoing," Mr. Canby grinned.

"My mother's gonna kill me!" Shelley breathed.

"*Your* mother!" Faith closed her eyes in dreaded anticipation. "Mine will skin me alive. After she boils me in oil."

The reporters furiously scribbled in their notebooks as Michael attempted unsuccessfully to calm everyone down. But at that point, it was totally useless. The situation had degenerated into a free-for-all, and only the sound of a lone police siren, cutting into the noise, made any difference at all.

In another instant, Sheriff Sackett and his men had arrived on the scene. Greenleaf only had three squad cars, but they were all present and accounted for. The Greenleaf police — all eight of them — jumped out of the cars, their guns drawn.

"I don't believe it!" Sheriff Sackett laughed when he saw what was going on. "This is what I got the emergency call about?"

"Sheriff, do your duty," Mr. Canby directed him as the cameras started rolling again and the reporters craned forward with their mikes. "Arrest these girls for criminal trespass."

"For what?" The sheriff scratched his head.

"Not to mention disturbing the peace." Mr. Canby folded his arms and stared directly at Dana, who gave him a weak little smile. This was certainly going further than anyone had intended it to.

"Now just a minute, Mr. Canby." Alison used her most conciliatory tone. "I think we can settle all this without resorting to any extreme measures. I've informed Ms. Allardyce, and she's on her way. She should be here at any moment. In the meantime, girls, if you'll just unlock yourselves . . ." she glared at them, ". . . I think we can avoid any further difficulties."

Nobody moved; nobody spoke; nobody budged an inch.

"Go ahead, Sheriff. I want the ringleaders in jail. That's this front line of girls." Mr. Canby aimed his gloved finger at them as though it were the barrel of a machine gun. "And, I would assume, the front line at all the other buildings as well. Lock up everyone who appears to be in charge."

"Well, I. . . ." The sheriff, who knew most of the girls Mr. Canby had indicated, clearly had no idea what he should do. He'd never run into a situation like this before. "Girls, do you think you could come along with me for a couple hours?" he asked politely. Then he turned to Mr. Canby. "I've only got two cells, and I'm not gonna shove 'em in there, so they'll just have to sit around my office," he said firmly.

He looked at Mr. Canby one last time. "You really serious about pressing charges?" Mr. Canby nodded emphatically. "Well, then, Edgar," he told one of his men, "clip them chains and put these ten kids in the cars. We'll have to come back to the other buildings later. Sorry, girls," he said when Edgar went to work. "This sure isn't my notion of how to conduct the duties of my office."

As Dana, Casey, Faith, and Shelley were

escorted to the first squad car in line, the other girls on the steps and porch booed and hissed. The prisoners walked with their heads held high, despite their incredibly low spirits.

"At least it's warm in here," Casey whispered when they were locked into the squad car. The back doors had no handles.

The roommates looked at her in disbelief. "Casey, shut up," Dana grumbled. Then she sat back against the seat. All she could think of was how lucky she was not to have that monster, Owen Canby, for a father. If she ever saw Chris again, that would be the first thing she would tell him.

CHAPTER ELEVEN

There were forty of them, all told, when the squad cars finally parked in front of the jail an hour later.

"That's as many as we could get in the last load, boss," Edgar told Sheriff Sackett. "Is it enough?"

"It'll have to do." The sheriff scratched his head and looked at the assembled girls, who were sitting on the floor and on any available surface around the tiny office. Mary Sackett, the sheriff's wife, who'd come in to clean as she did every Saturday morning, was running around making pots of coffee and hot chocolate on the two little burners in the kitchen area and trying to see that everyone was comfortable. In between chores, she clucked loudly about the horrible man who'd insisted that these poor innocents be subjected to such an awful experience.

"Thank heaven we didn't have anyone in the drunk tank," she said to her husband when she went home to make lunch for forty. "The very thought of these lovely girls in the jail makes my blood boil. Why, they could be scarred for life!"

"Only after my mom hears about this," Faith muttered, pacing the floor. "*Then* I'll be scarred!"

"How's she going to hear?" Shelley demanded. "I mean, we may get some good local coverage tonight in Boston, but it's not the kind of story they'd run in another city."

"I wouldn't be too sure about keeping it under wraps," Dana sighed, her elbows propped on her knees as she sat in the corner. "My Aunt Harriet lives in Boston, remember. If she sees us on the news or reads about us in the paper, she'll call my mom in New York. And my mom might do your folks the favor of calling Washington, D.C. and Pine Bluff, Iowa, just to make sure nobody's going to feel left out," she added with a sarcastic smirk.

"Yeah, and then there's the wonderful Associated Press," Joan Barr said helpfully. "They love to pick up human interest stories from the major papers and sell them to little rags in Nebraska and Wyoming, or wherever. Even Pine Bluff."

"Oh, no! My father will never speak to me again," Shelley wailed. "People don't get arrested in Pine Bluff. It's just . . . not done!"

"What are you people griping about?" Casey huffed, taking a sip of her cocoa. "We wanted publicity, right? We thought of the consequences. All we didn't know was that he'd have us arrested. That's all."

"That's all, she says," Faith grunted. "Just because your parents are flying around the world most of the time collecting art, you escape scot-free. What do you think's going to happen to us now?"

The four girls looked over at the sheriff, who was puzzling over a pile of forms on his desk. "Go on, ask him," Dana prodded Shelley.

Shelley cleared her throat and got up off the floor, walking around the various clusters of girls to reach the desk. "Ah, excuse me, Sheriff," she smiled politely. "But can you tell us what this really means? Um, do we get a record for life or something?"

Sheriff Sackett muttered something and then shrugged at her. "Now listen here. I don't like this one bit, and I've said it before. But Edgar just brought me the forms." He waved them in front of her. "If you ask me, which you didn't, but I'll tell you anyhow, that rich businessman has his nerve signing a complaint against a bunch of kids who didn't do a thing but sit on some steps. Besides, how does he know which ones are guilty and which ones Edgar just picked up because he didn't know any better? I think the whole thing is a load of tommyrot."

"But now that he's formally signed something. . . . ?" Shelley persisted.

"Well, I gotta set bail, 'cause you been

arrested. But with a bail bond, you can get off for ten percent of the price. I guess your head-mistress can pay that when she gets here."

"Ms. Allardyce!" Casey, who was listening intently to this conversation, suddenly smacked her forehead with one palm. "We forgot all about her. She's going to expel us. I can't figure out which is worse — having an arrest record, or getting expelled from Canby Hall. And we didn't *do* anything! That's the lousy part. We didn't even get to have any fun being bad." She pouted and started pacing the floor with Faith.

"I think we should all discuss this," Dana began, "and talk about what we're going to do and say when they come to get us. Hey, everybody!"

The murmuring tapered off as Dana called for their attention. The girls, some of whom looked terribly frightened and others of whom looked like this was life's greatest adventure so far, turned to face one of their leaders.

"I just want to tell you," Dana began, "you've all been great, and whatever happens after this —" But just then, the door to the jail opened, and Chris Canby stormed through it.

"What in heaven's name!" He looked in astonishment at Dana and then at the throng of girls. "This is unbelievable."

"That's what we thought," Dana said to him between clenched teeth. "But your father proved us wrong."

"Dana, please, you don't think that I condone. . . ." He stopped, seeing that he had a rapt audience, and took her by the arm. "Is there somewhere we can talk?"

The sheriff thumbed his finger toward the back. "Cells are thataway," he nodded.

Chris paid no attention to Dana's clear reluctance to walk with him and practically dragged her toward the corridor that led to the two cells.

"Well, isn't this cozy?" she asked sarcastically, when they were standing outside the metal bars. "I've only seen jail cells on T.V. My education has suddenly been expanded."

"Please don't be like this. I had no idea my father would go this far. You have to know that I may have been with him all the way on every other step of this sale, but now, I wouldn't give him the time of day."

"He doesn't need it. He has a beeper, remember?" Dana knew she was being hateful, but Chris was the closest target on which she could take out her rage and frustration.

"This is not my fault, Dana!"

"I know, I know," she relented. "But if you don't mind my saying so, I never want to see your father again. And I really don't think we should see each other, either."

His handsome face looked pained, and those piercing eyes pleaded with her for a little understanding. "I don't blame you for wanting to rub all the Canbys out of your life, but give it some time, would you, Dana?

I know you and I have had our differences about progress and the world of high finance, but my ideas about those things are just part of me. I care about other things, too. I was brought up believing the party line about money, you know, and sometimes it takes an experience like this to kind of wake you up. I guess I did think the sun rose and set on my dad's empire for a while. Well, it never occurred to me how many people he trampled to get that empire spinning around his axis. He's a very ruthless man, and not always nice." He stopped and ran a hand through his wild, red hair. "That was a very hard thing for me to say."

She couldn't be angry at him anymore. She put one hand on his cheek and nodded in agreement. "It sure was."

"So now the problem is how to get you guys out of here without a record. I mean, your headmistress will probably dock you all for some unconscionable period of time, but that should be the worst of it. I consider it my job to get my father to drop the charges."

"What did he say when you saw him?" Dana asked anxiously.

"I didn't. I mean, I heard the news on the car radio — that's why I rushed right down here."

"Well, where is he?"

"Probably doing the inventory. I can catch him at Canby Hall, and then, I guess, it's up to me to prevail on his better nature."

Dana gave a snort of disbelief. "This *is* his better nature."

Chris made a face. "You know him pretty well, don't you?"

"Not as well as you. And I don't envy you one bit."

For a minute, Chris looked like a little lost boy, but then he pulled himself together and started to walk back down the corridor toward the front office. "I'm going to Canby Hall to try to find him and persuade him. As long as Ms. Allardyce pries you loose from Sheriff Sackett, you'll be okay." He turned to her at the door. "Won't you?"

She smiled bravely. "I guess. Sure."

But when they stepped back in the front room, they were totally unprepared for the sight that greeted them. An old man, dressed in rumpled overalls and a torn wool hat, was turning out his pockets on Sheriff Sackett's desk. Shelley was shaking her head in wonder at him.

"Dana, oh, come here!" she said when she spotted her roommate. "This is Mr. Sampton — remember I told you Tom and I met him at Pizza Pete's? He's come to bail us out."

"Now just a second here." Mr. Sampton nodded perfunctorily at Dana and went back to his counting. "You want a hundred clams for the forty of 'em — that what you said?" he asked the sheriff again.

"Well, it's ten percent of the bail, so I guess it's gotta be the full hundred. Cary, if you don't have it, I'll stake you to it," the sheriff said, trying to sound generous. He opened his desk and began rummaging around for the petty cash box. "I'm not supposed to, but what the heck? I couldn't live with myself if I didn't."

"Naw, I got it here somewhere." Mr. Sampton put a collection of one-dollar bills on the desk and a mountain of change on top of that. He came up with a few stamps and some loose keys, then found two twenties in his shirt pocket.

"This is just wonderful of you, Mr. Sampton," Faith said gratefully. "We're going to pay you back out of our fund-raising money this month — we promise." She looked at Casey and Dana, so touched that she couldn't say any more. The poor guy looked like he had barely enough to keep himself in shoelaces, and here he was, bailing them out! It was nice to see that even in a world that housed people like Owen Canby, there were golden ones like Cary Sampton to make up for it.

"Here, I got it!" he proclaimed triumphantly, pulling off one shoe. He pried up the tattered lining and carefully removed three very old twenty-dollar bills. "I knew I'd stashed that somewhere."

Everyone in the room burst into spontaneous applause, and Cheryl began to sing, "For He's A Jolly Good Fellow." The others joined in, clapping to their own song. They were right in the middle of "Which nobody can deny," when the door opened again. In walked Patrice Allardyce followed by Alison and Michael.

A deathlike pall descended upon the room. Everyone's eyes were glued to the headmistress' face, which was stony and rigid. In her straight blue wool coat and neat felt hat, she looked positively military.

"You have all gravely disappointed me," Ms. Allardyce said softly. "I asked for your cooperation in my absence, and instead, I find a scandal to rival any that Canby Hall has ever known in its entire history. I don't quite know how we will live it down, but we will certainly try." Her voice was terribly hushed, painfully quiet. Dana kept wishing she would yell a little — it would make the criticism so much easier to take.

"Ma'am," Sheriff Sackett mumbled, "I just gotta tell you that you have some pretty plucky girls here."

"I have never doubted their courageous spirits," Ms. Allardyce told him. "What I wonder is if they have any common sense. When we return to campus," she said, opening her purse, "I will expect to see the organizers of this demonstration at my house immediately. I have been led to believe that there are eight of you. As for the rest," she looked at the timid troops huddled on the floor, "this experience has probably taught you something, but being docked from all

social events for the next month may teach
you more."

She turned back to the sheriff, very busi-
nesslike now. "I understand that bail has been
set at one thousand dollars, of which you expect to be paid ten percent on a bond."

"That's okay, ma'am," Cary Sampton piped
up. "Bail's been taken care of."

She looked at the collection of bills and
coins on the table, then back at the rumpled
old man before her. "It's very kind of you, I'm
sure, but this is the school's expense."

"You folks are having enough worries," Mr.
Sampton insisted. "Sheriff, just wipe that
money off the table and enough said about it."

"No," Ms. Allardyce persisted, with finality.
"The girls' bail is my responsibility." She
took out her wallet and produced two fifty-
dollar bills, which she handed to the sheriff.
"You may send the receipt to the school," she
told him. Then she turned to Mr. Sampton.
"And I do thank you, sir, whoever you are,
for kindly offering to pay it in my absence. I
can see that the girls are greatly indebted to
you. I have the school van waiting outside.
Would everyone please put on her things and
begin lining up."

With that, she marched to the door, leaving Alison and Michael to herd everybody out
of the jail. Alison put a sympathetic hand on
Casey's and Faith's shoulders.

"Whew!" Casey breathed, sticking her hat

on her head. "Did she eat nails for breakfast, or what?"

"Sweetie, she's been through a lot lately. I think it's like her whole world has just fallen apart. Don't blame her too much."

"I wish she wouldn't blame *us* so much," Faith sighed as she started for the van.

Shelley took her parka off the floor and came back to Mr. Sampton, who was reluctantly picking his money up off the table. "She should have thanked you more for your generosity," Shelley said softly, "but you know what it meant to us. You're a real pal, Mr. Sampton."

"Don't bother your head. I been looking for that stash, anyhow. Now I found it. Keep your noses clean, now," he called as the girls left the jail.

Chris and Dana said good-bye at the door. "She's a tough one," Chris grinned after Ms. Allardyce. "Don't let her get you down, no matter what she says. And listen, Dana, I'm going to see you even if you are docked for a month — after I prove myself to you by getting my dad to drop the charges. I have my ingenious ways," he teased.

She found it hard to manage a smile, so she just nodded and followed the others to the van. When the doors closed behind her, Chris was standing on the sidewalk beside his car, looking up at her.

The trip back to campus was awkward, to

say the least. No one wanted to make chit-chat with Ms. Allardyce, along for the ride, and of course, the eight girls who were about to be called on the carpet were wondering how bad it was going to be. There was no traffic on the road, so they were back and through the Canby Hall gates in no time.

"I think I'd rather be back in jail," Faith muttered as Ms. Allardyce led the way to her house.

"Let's get it over with," Dana shrugged, waiting on the path so that Ellie, Cheryl, Joan, and Ginny could catch up with her, Casey, and Shelley.

"What can she give us besides more docking?" Shelley whispered, watching Ms. Allardyce unlock her front door and walk inside.

"Fifty lashes," Casey said decisively. "She's in that kind of mood."

But the girls were surprised and astounded when they hesitantly followed Ms. Allardyce into the foyer. The headmistress simply removed her coat, hung it neatly in the closet, and then, wonder of wonders, smiled at them.

"I won't keep you long," she sighed, going over to her fireplace and striking a match under the kindling that had already been laid. A flame sparked into life and caught.

"I hope you understand that I had to disapprove of what you did, and I wanted the others to see that this sort of behavior can't be tolerated. But with you, I must be honest. I'm very proud of the way you decided to defend the school. I probably wouldn't have felt this way a month or so ago, but I suppose we all grow up and maybe even become more flexible as we grow older. You girls have taught me a great deal in my tenure here as headmistress. I will always remember you fondly, and with great esteem."

And then, the steely, austere headmistress of Canby Hall opened her arms to the girls and collected all eight of them in a huge embrace. They didn't know whether to laugh or cry — they were that dumbfounded.

"Now get back to your dorms, all of you," she said when the whole scene threatened to become more emotional than any of them could handle. "You're docked, remember," she said in her usual no-nonsense voice.

As they were straggling out the door, they heard her say quite distinctly, "You are permitted, however, to watch the six o'clock news on your lounge televisions. There may be something on of particular interest to all of us." Then she turned and walked back to the fire, and they couldn't see the tears glistening in her eyes.

CHAPTER TWELVE

At six o'clock, the dining hall was completely empty. This was an unprecedented event, but nobody took any notice of it because they were all glued to the T.V. sets in the three dorms. Tom had zoomed over on his motorcycle right after school when he saw the late edition of the *Chronicle*. By now, the two-page spread, complete with pictures and a headline larger than the girls could have hoped for, was hanging on the Baker bulletin board.

" 'Canby Girls Struggle For Right Against Corporate Might'," Shelley repeated in an excited delirium as Tom worked on the T.V.'s fine tuning. The WBZ anchorwoman had just begun the local broadcast. "I hope these guys say something as nice."

"I hope my Aunt Harriet went to a movie," Dana muttered. Then everyone listened with eager anticipation as the lead stories about war in the Middle East and the President's news conference rolled by.

"But you haven't said what Allardyce did to you." Pamela Young broke the silence when the first commercial came on the air. "What's the punishment?" She looked at Faith, who shrugged mysteriously and at Shelley, who moved a little closer to Tom.

"Let's put it this way," Dana said non-committally. "It wasn't what we expected. But we're going to have to live with it. Shh, Pamela, it's starting again," she hushed her as the anchor's intense face came back on the air.

There was one short story about the renovation of a down-and-out block in the North End by its residents, and then, it was the girls' turn. "Look!" Eileen Davis squealed as the first picture of Canby Hall's massive gates came on screen, "it's us!"

"The institution of Canby Hall," read the off-camera reporter, "has existed on Horace Canby's estate in Greenleaf, Massachusetts since 1897, when the philanthropist/business-man founded a secondary school for young ladies in memory of his daughter, Julia, who had died the previous year on a trip to Europe. The school's academic standards have always been excellent, and the administration's belief in encouraging young women to think for themselves, to dare to tackle the impossible, has always been commendable.

Today, the students did just that: They took a stand against corporate enterprise and gave Owen Canby, the millionaire entrepreneur, a real run for his money."

"This is great!" Casey was jumping up and down in her armchair. "They're behind us all the way!"

The cameras panned over the girls, showing their posters, and then zoomed in on the first row, capturing Casey, Faith, Shelley, and Dana as they were about to start answering questions.

The extraordinary thing about the two-minute piece was the way it had been edited. Mr. Canby, who'd seemed completely in control at the scene, was shown pulling at his gloves and licking his lips every time a reporter pushed a mike in front of him. The girls all sounded articulate and self-assured, perfectly prepared to combat the enemy. The best part, of course, was when the sheriff and his men got there and chaos broke out. The Data-Tech people looked like clowns, scrambling to get into their van, and poor Edgar seemed so put-upon when he was clipping the girls' chains, you had to feel sorry for him. The news segment ended with the reporter standing in front of the wishing pool.

"Horace Canby had a dream," she said slowly. "A dream that he felt would last over time. But these days, time is money, and sometimes we forget that there are more precious things at stake — like our children and their futures. The students of Canby Hall are now involved in a massive fund-raising drive to keep their institution going, somewhere, somehow. Maybe, if they get a little help from their friends and can manage to stay out of jail, they might just keep that dream going for another ninety years."

"Boy," Tom said, hugging Shelley close, "I wish I'd been a fly on the wall in Canby's house tonight. His face must be green now."

"Hmm," Faith sighed philosophically. "But have we changed anything? That's the big one." She was about to say something else when every phone in the phone bank began ringing madly. Heather and Ellie popped up to answer them all.

"The only way anything's going to change is for Pamela's mother and some of the others to come through with the dough immediately," Casey said, staring straight at Pamela, who was staring at her fingernails. "That way, we'll have time to lease a piece of property for next semester."

"Faith!" Ellie called. "Phone for you. It's long distance," she warned, covering the mouthpiece. "Must be your mom."

"Ouch!" Faith took a deep breath and put the phone to her ear. "Hi? Hi, mom, how are you?"

Mrs. Thompson's deep voice boomed from the other end of the line. "Sweetheart, now I

want to know if this is true. Harold and
Martha's boy, Jack, is at college up near you,
and he called to say there was this piece in
the paper tonight about a demonstration at
your school. He says some of the girls got
arrested and that there was this tiny picture
showing one black face in the first row who
looked an awful lot like you."

"Well, it's true. I went to jail. But as you
can see," Faith continued cheerily, "I'm home
now. Everything's okay, mom. And everybody
seems to agree that we were right about what
we did."

"Darling," her mother sounded like she
was trying not to scold. "We had a lot of
conversations in the past when your father was
alive about getting into trouble with the law.
You know my stand on that, regardless of
who's right and who's wrong."

Faith did remember. But how else should
her mother feel? She prided herself on having
raised three good kids in a pretty tough neighborhood. "Mom, I wouldn't do anything il-
legal — ever. But sometimes, you have to do
things you wouldn't do under ordinary circumstances. I mean, you and Dad marched on
Washington with Martin Luther King in 1963
— you used to tell me and Sarah and Richie
about that march all the time. I guess, tech-
nically, our protest was just like that."

Mrs. Thompson was silent for a moment,
and then she said, "I feel you know what

you're doing. I just hope that it gives you the
results you're after. Don't be too terribly disappointed if it doesn't. I love you, darling."

"I love you, Mom." They each hung up,
and Faith felt a gigantic boulder roll off her
shoulder as she did so. Her mother wasn't
mad! She was about to walk away when the
phone she'd been using rang again.

"Hello, Baker House. Yes, Mrs. Granick,
Andrea's right here. I'll call her." Faith peered
around the room until she'd spotted Andrea
and went over to get her. "Next," she said
wryly. Then she added, "Don't worry. Mine
wasn't half bad."

The calls kept coming all night and all the
next morning. There were emergency arrivals
of parents who'd heard from somebody who'd
heard from somebody and had driven all
night, determined to take their babies home,
out of that awful environment. By now, of
course, every family had received Ms. Allardyce's announcement that the school would
be closing in June, and the more panicky types
seemed to figure that the arrest was the last
straw.

"I don't know what I'd do if my parents
told me to fly home," Shelley mused the next
day as she dug into a very large breakfast. She
was ravenous, having only been able to
scrounge some leftover fruit salad the night
before. "I'd protest," she said decisively, taking a large bite of toast.

"My mother won't get hysterical," Dana said with an assurance she really didn't feel. "She's very cool, very together." It was at this very second, of course, that the cook came out of the kitchen to say that they were transferring Dana's call from Baker to the pay phone in the dining hall lobby.

"Oh, well," Casey shrugged. "It's been swell."

"Casey!" Faith reprimanded her.

"Look," Casey told her as Dana went solemnly to answer the phone. "I come from one of these liberal, understanding, openminded households. But I know just how they can clamp down when they reach their limit."

"Dana's mother wouldn't make her come home. That's absurd," Shelley insisted. "It would have to be a major catastrophe, like . . . I don't know, like Owen Canby firing all the teachers, or something equally disastrous. A little arrest and some notoriety wouldn't do it."

They all looked over at Dana, standing in the corridor, holding the phone at a distance. Then, she put it to her ear.

"Darling? Did I get through?" Carol Morrison's clear voice sang out over the wires from New York.

"Yes, I'm here, Mom. How are you?"

"How am I? What a question. How are *you*, little jailbird?"

She was joking! Everything was okay. "I'm

great. So, you've heard," Dana nodded at the
phone.

"How could I help it? Listen, babe, I never
called when I got that letter from your headmistress, because I thought, what's to discuss?
I figured you'd just move back at the end of
the term and start public school here in the
fall. But I've given it some thought since Harriet called last night — dear Harriet, never
misses a trick! — and I think it might be
better if you just packed and came home
now. We can get you into Academic High
right away."

"Oh, no, Mom!" Dana was scandalized.

"Sweetie, I was just going to come like a
thief in the night and arrive on your doorstep
this morning. But then, I decided, well, she's
an adult; I don't have to play nursemaid. Still
and all, I am your mother, and I'm worried
about you. And, I don't want you to fall behind and miss all the important end of junior
year stuff. It just makes more sense this way. I
mean, Canby Hall must be a mess right now.
None of you concentrating on your work, and
all this worry about that lousy guy who's closing you down. It just seems right to me to
have you home."

"Not to me. Not to us. Mom, Shelley and
Faith and I are the backbone of this fight. We
can't give up now. I mean, all we've lost so far
is the property. We can still have a Canby
Hall next year, but it's going to take us the

next three months at least to get the money
we need and find a new space and everything.
We're going to classes and studying and taking tests just the way we always were — it's
just that saving Canby Hall is our new extracurricular activity. If I go home now, I'm a
traitor — to myself as well as to everybody
else. Please don't make me."

Carol Morrison took a deep breath. "I don't
know. I'll think about it. And I'm going to
call your father in Hawaii and discuss it with
him. If he agrees with me that you should
come home, Dana, that's it."

There was silence between them for a moment, and then Mrs. Morrison asked, "So what
was jail like?"

"Not bad," Dana said with a small laugh.
"Please don't worry about me, Mom."

"Are you kidding? I'll worry about you
till the day I die. That's what love is, kid. All
right, be cheery. Talk to you soon."

As Dana hung up, she was only mildly
worried. Her father wouldn't insist that she
leave. She just knew it.

"Well?" Casey looked at her expectantly as
she walked back to their table. Faith and Shelley, however, were bent over a slip of paper
and were laughing hysterically.

"It was okay. What's going on?" Dana asked
her two ridiculous roommates.

"Shelley's parents sent a telegram — Joanne
just brought it over from the office. Here,
read!" Faith scooted it across the table.

* * *

"Slugger," (that was Shelley's brothers' nick-name for her)

> "You used to be our sweet girl scout, the darling of Pine Bluff
> But now you've left us, you've turned out
> To be so rough and tough.
> We see from all the papers that your cause was right and true,
> The money men and bankers can't just walk all over you.
> We love you, baby, that's the truth, but now we've got one plea,
> Could you stay out of jail — we can't make bail — your parents beg hope-fully?
> P.S. Your brothers want the autograph of some Eastern desperado . . . if you know any. (Mom)
> P.P.S. If I ever hear of your pulling a stunt like this for any other reason, I swear I'll tan your hide myself. (Dad)."

"They are thoroughly incredible," Shelley marveled, folding the telegram in half and tucking it into the back pocket of her slacks. "I never expected a reaction like this."

"I guess we got what we wanted," Casey said sensibly. "I mean, all our press was so good, *we* looked good. We didn't look like a bunch of rowdy kids going up against the staid establishment. I just wish Owen Canby had half a heart."

"Me, too," Dana said. She was thinking about Chris now, and wondering if he'd been able to work any miracles on his father. She decided to call him after dinner and find out.

"Guess we better get to first class," Faith sighed when the bell rang. "From now on, it's class and study, and do whatever fund-raising we can from the Baker phones. Docked for a month — whew!"

"Listen, it's better than being yanked out of school. Did you see, Toni Eberhardt was driven away this morning," Casey said as they took their trays over to the tray return.

"And Andrea's scheduled to go this weekend," Shelley said sadly. "A couple of other girls, too, from what I hear. I hate the thought of our forces being so depleted."

"You talk like this is a war," Casey said.

"Of course it is," Dana smiled. "And much to Owen Canby's dismay, we just won the biggest battle so far." She stuck her lower lip out and made a fist. "All we have to do is keep on winning them."

The following evening, after Study Hours were over, the committee had a meeting in Room 407. The WBZ broadcast and the local newspaper coverage had already brought an avalanche of mail into the administrative offices, all addressed to the Save Canby Hall Committee. Some of the letters were just statements from well-wishers, but many included checks, ranging in amounts from $20 to $500.

"And I talked to somebody at the station who said they've got piles of letters, too. They're shipping some bags over as soon as they get a chance," Cheryl explained. "If this keeps up, we really could come up with the three million!"

"Well, I kind of doubt that, but maybe enough to lease a building," Joan said, doing some quick calculations. "I think some of us should go to work on that immediately. Find out what's available in the nearby vicinity that could serve as dorms and classrooms. We could call some realtors and —"

She was interrupted by the sound of something hitting the window. They all looked over to see what it was, then went back to the drawing board.

"So as I was saying —" The noise came again, a loud spray of pebbles grazing the glass.

"What the . . . ?" Dana got up, went to the window and opened it, looking around carefully.

"Hey, Dana!" A hoarse whisper came from the vicinity of the bushes near Baker's back door.

"Who's there?" She peered into the darkness, unable to see a thing.

"It's me, your friendly local kook. Who else would go prowling the campus at this hour?" Chris stuck his head up out of the bush, then ducked back down again. "It's thorny in here."

"I'll bet." Dana wanted to laugh, but didn't dare. "How did you get in through the gates?"

"I didn't. I jogged down from Oakley and cut through the maple grove. I'm freezing!"

Casey, Faith, and Shelley appeared at the window, and Chris waved to them half-heartedly. "I suppose you couldn't throw me down a nice hot cup of coffee?" he asked hopefully.

" 'Fraid not. Got any news?" Casey demanded.

"I got my father to drop the charges. None of you has to go through life with a police record."

"Hooray!" Shelley began to yell, then clapped a hand over her mouth. She knew she could get Chris in terrible trouble if he was caught.

"You're a genius," Dana said admiringly. "How'd you'd get him to relent?"

"I'm not sure, really. But something's going on. Ever since that newscast, he's been acting weird. I know he's a sore loser, but it's something else, too. I can't put my finger on it."

"Anyhow, you did it, you great person, you," Casey grinned. "When we're let out of prison next month, we'll treat you to a pizza." Then she looked over at Dana, who was smiling down at Chris with a really goony expression on her face. She got the hint and bodily pulled Faith and Shelley into the room, back to the other girls. It was clear that Chris and Dana wanted a quiet word together.

"Thank you," Dana murmured down to him. "You're a wonderful friend."

"Yeah, sort of. Hey, Juliet, I wish you had some kind of balcony I could climb up on."

"Me, too, Romeo." She blushed as she said it, and was glad of the darkness that covered her embarrassment. "I suppose all formal thank yous will have to wait."

"Too bad."

A knock at the door of Room 407 ended the sweet words abruptly. "Dana, tell him to scat," Casey hissed. "There's somebody here. Just a minute!" she called out.

"Chris, get lost. We've got company," Dana said hastily, closing the window. Her cheeks were rosy when she walked back to the others, but she knew it wasn't because of the cold. "Okay, all clear," she whispered to Ellie, who opened the door, trying to pretend that nothing out of the ordinary had been going on.

"Alison!" Faith rushed to the housemother as soon as she saw her white face. "What is it?"

"I have to sit down. Can I sit down?" She plopped on the mattress that served as Shelley's bed. One of the girls handed her a Tab from the pile on the window, but she waved it away.

"Can you talk? What happened?" Dana demanded.

"The whole school will know tomorrow, but I just couldn't keep it to myself overnight." Alison looked at each of them, suddenly seeming very young and lost. "It's Ms. Allardyce," she said in a rush. "She just called to tell me she's resigning."

CHAPTER THIRTEEN

Everyone shouted at once, except for Dana, who slumped on her mattress in an agony of realization.

"She can't resign! Not now!" Shelley exclaimed.

"What kind of a person *is* she, anyway!" Casey demanded.

Joan and Cheryl both moaned, "Oh, no!" and Ginny and Ellie started babbling incoherently. Faith, who felt her ears burning with indignant rage, yelled, "Well, she has her nerve, to abandon us now."

"I must say, I've never really understood what makes our headmistress tick," Alison said slowly, "but this blows my mind. Well, thanks for letting me unburden myself. I guess I can't stop you from spreading this all over Baker, maybe all over the school, but she's having another one of her famous early morning assemblies tomorrow, so it really doesn't matter. I don't think anything matters anymore."

"That means it's finished. There's no hope." Dana's quiet voice cut into the maelstrom. "It means we all have to go home and just start life over again, as if Canby Hall had never existed."

Alison moved over to Dana's bed and put her arm around the stricken girl as the others looked on, feeling Dana's pain as their own. "That's not so. What you've done here is nothing short of miraculous. You've been brave and faithful and true to your cause, and I think this experience was an important one — for all of us. You don't always get the goodies, though, Dana, and that's the sad part. You can work and slave and give up everything for your goal, and somebody still beats you. It only means you have to try even harder the next time."

Alison got up and walked wearily to the door. "I have to buzz the other houseparents and faculty, let them know about the meeting tomorrow. Get some sleep, everybody. See you in the auditorium at eight-thirty."

When the door had closed behind her, the girls all looked at one another, trying to think of something constructive or comforting to say. But they were all talked out, all thought out. It seemed like this had been going on forever. Slowly, one by one, the other girls left, and the roommates sat together on Dana's mattress.

"I don't think I can fall asleep," Shelley said.

"Me either," Faith sighed. "Want to play cards or something?"

They tried that for a while, but nobody was paying much attention, so at midnight, they gave up and turned out the lights. It was a long time until morning.

The auditorium filled quickly. News had, of course, spread like a brush fire, and everyone now dreaded the anticlimax of the actual announcement. There seemed to be a general feeling of ill-will toward Ms. Allardyce, too, and that didn't make things easier. Under the current of murmuring, there was a lot of heavy thinking going on — girls thinking about home, about their parents, about the future. It was scary.

"Good morning." Ms. Allardyce's voice cut through the fog that permeated the room. She looked very thin and tall that morning, dressed in a smart black knit dress with a cream collar and cuffs. Her face held no trace of the emotion of the other day, but she did look haggard, as though she hadn't slept in weeks.

"I've brought you all together this morning to announce my resignation — as I suppose you already know," she added, with what might, in anyone else, have passed for a wink. She might be steely and austere, but she knew her girls. If there was a way for a rumor to spread around Canby Hall, it would.

"Before you all hurl rotten tomatoes at me, let me explain myself. Clearly, I'm not leaving here. They'll have to drag me out bodily when they finally take over the school. What I am doing is lodging a formal protest, much in the same way as you girls did the other day. I'm informing Mr. Owen Canby, his board of directors, and the press that I cannot, in all good conscience, maintain the position of headmistress and chief administrator of this school when they've pulled the rug right out from under us. Whatever Mr. Canby and his trustees decide from here on, I am not with them, and I do not wish to be associated with the takeover in any way, as I would be were I still in their employ."

There was an audible sigh of relief. The girls and faculty relaxed in their seats, waiting for her next words. The tide that had turned against her during the night had flowed right back — they were completely on her side.

"I am therefore going to stay on until the closing of the school, and afterward, if need be, as coordinator and acting principal. I will take no remuneration for these duties. I want you all to know that I will be available at any time to discuss any problem you may be having, whether it be transferring to another school or completing your year's assignments here. I will also be advising the faculty and writing references for all of them."

She leaned forward on the podium and for a moment, her face seemed subtly softer. "This is a terrible state of affairs. I love this school and I'm proud of what we've done to enhance its reputation over the years. If there is any way, any way at all, to keep this institution going in some new format, I intend to help to make it a possibility. It goes without saying that we'll have to change our name."

At this, everyone burst out laughing. It felt so good to let it all go, to exorcise the presence of Owen Canby who seemed to sit up there on the platform next to Ms. Allardyce, gloating in his success.

As Ms. Allardyce was trying to restore order so that she could go on, her secretary, Peggy, came trundling down the aisle of the auditorium, practically tripping over herself as she dragged a stack of old shoeboxes, tied up with a large piece of cord. She lugged the boxes onstage, then huffed her way up the steps to the headmistress, who was staring at her in great confusion. Everyone in the auditorium began buzzing.

"I'm sorry, I really am, Ms. Allardyce, but the boy said if I didn't interrupt you, he'd have to take them back again, and if he did, I'd be really sorry because this is what we've been waiting for. And since he wouldn't tell me what was in them — or in the note — I just had to take the chance." The flustered woman retrieved a rather crushed envelope from her jacket pocket. "I do apologize, to everyone, and if this is just some silly kid's idea of a trick, then you've got to forgive me. But, I don't know, I just had a feeling about him. You know when you get those feelings, and they won't go away?" She was so rattled, she couldn't stop talking. The whole audience was buzzing now, and Ms. Allardyce was starting to look exasperated.

"I haven't got time for this, Peggy," she said brusquely.

"I knew I shouldn't interrupt, but. . . ."

"Well, bring them over to my office. I'll deal with it when I have a chance."

Peggy hesitated. "It's probably nothing, but this kid drove up in his pickup and said I was to get hold of you immediately because you had to open these in front of the entire school. And I thought, what better opportunity than right now." She tentatively handed the envelope to her boss, who accepted it just so that she could get rid of this pesky nuisance and go on with what she'd been saying. When Peggy continued to stand there, Ms. Allardyce threw up her hands and finally ripped the envelope open with a look of cynical skepticism on her face. Inside was a piece of yellow legal paper, folded in thirds.

" 'This letter,' " she read into the microphone, " 'is for the entire student body and faculty, particularly for the Save Canby Hall Committee.' " She looked up at the assembled crowd, then back down at the note.

" 'When you're playing for high stakes, you

have to play every card you've got and some you haven't. This should do for the first year. After that, you're on your own.' " She turned the note over, looking for a signature, but there was none.

But clearly, her curiosity was piqued. She shrugged and bent down to slip the cord off the top shoebox. She did it gingerly, as though she feared there might be a bomb or something equally awful inside. As she pulled off the lid, the girls in the first row stood to get a better view. But even those whose view was totally blocked couldn't miss the headmistress' reaction. She lost her balance and tumbled backward, knocking over the box.

Bundles of money lay in profusion on the floor. New bills and old bills, some tied up with rubber bands, some in paper money holders. The amazing sight brought the entire room to its feet, cheering and applauding.

"Open the others!" somebody yelled.

"Where's the math department? Let's start counting!" came another cry.

Girls were hugging each other and dashing into the aisles for a better view when Ms. Allardyce opened the next box, then the next. When all six shoeboxes lay in a line on the stage floor, the sound in the hall was deafening.

Faith and Shelley were pounding Dana on the back, because she was laughing and coughing at the same time. "We're saved!" Faith sobbed. "Somebody saved us."

"But who?" Shelley demanded. Then she went back to the little jig she was doing in front of her seat.

Dana's mind was going like fury. "Could Chris have something to do with this?"

"How could he?" Faith scoffed. "Unless he's holding his father for ransom."

"No, not Chris." Shelley shook her head. "Where's Pamela?"

They looked behind them to where Pamela sat with Heather and Mary Beth Grover. She looked absolutely shell-shocked.

"Is it your mother?" Faith leaned over the seat back and screamed through the hubbub.

"I don't know. I certainly don't think she'd send shoeboxes." Pamela shook her neat blonde head. "Anyway, she's in Europe. I don't get it."

The girls were almost too delirious to care where the bounty had come from at this point. They could see the incredulity on Ms. Allardyce's face, and that made them laugh, too, because their once emotionless headmistress was just as giddy and loopy as they were.

The pandemonium went on for another good ten minutes, and then, finally, Ms. Allardyce waved both hands above her head for order. "I . . . I'm speechless. Does anyone know anything about this? Anyone on the committee?"

"Beats us," Casey yelled. "But ain't it great?"

Everyone pounded their feet on the floor

in unison and wouldn't stop until Ms. Allardyce tapped the mike for silence. "Well then, I'm going to have Peggy get this right over to the accountant's office so he can go through it and total it. We'll have to find out what the legal ramifications of this are, but I'm not going to worry about that right now. This looks to me like a great deal of money. Perhaps millions — certainly enough to take care of us for the next year. You're all dismissed — and have a wonderful day," she added needlessly.

As Alison herded her girls outside into the clear winter sunshine, she spotted Michael, who came up to give first her, and then as many girls as happened to be within his arms' reach, a gigantic hug. "Remember I said it wasn't time to quit?" Michael sang out. "Somebody up there loves us."

"I wish I knew who. Whom," Dana muttered.

"I have this weird idea," Shelley mused, but nobody was really listening.

"I think we should run some kind of thank you to our anonymous contributor in the *Chronicle*," Faith said as they walked along the path. "It couldn't cost very much." Then she bent over double and laughed hysterically. "What am I saying? We could buy the newspaper now!"

"No, we can't squander a cent of this," Alison said. "I think Ms. Allardyce is going to make sure that every penny goes right into a special Save Canby Hall fund. I saw her and Peggy rush right out of the auditorium a few seconds ago, hauling all that loot, and I'll bet she was on her way right back to her house to get some realty people on the phone — see what we can get for next year. And that's fine, too."

"Well, will you look who the cat dragged in." Casey pointed over toward the head-mistress' house. Parked in the drive outside was the notorious blue Mercedes belonging to none other than Owen Canby.

"Now what does he want, I wonder?" Shelley said.

The familiar tall figure emerged from the back seat, trying to keep his hat on in the stiff breeze. He walked slowly and steadily to Ms. Allardyce's door and rang the bell.

"I wish we could tell him." Faith rubbed her hands in glee.

"C'mon, let's just take a peek," Dana said mischievously. "Maybe we can catch a glimpse of his face when Ms. Allardyce greets him at the door with the news."

"You kids can go peer in the windows if you like. I'm an adult," Michael said, regret-fully strolling away toward the library as Mr. Canby disappeared inside the house. Almost as an afterthought, Michael grabbed Alison's hand. "Let's leave the kids to their moment of glory," he said softly. She nodded, then waved good-bye to the girls as they trundled off together.

"What do you think?" Dana asked, staring at the house.

"I think we should do it. *We're* not adults," Casey pointed out.

"Oh, all right," Faith concurred. A nod from Shelley and the four of them were off, giggling and shoving each other, racing up the path toward Ms. Allardyce's house. They were trying to shush each other when the front door was flung open. A very triumphant Ms. Allardyce stood there grinning — something none of the girls had ever seen her do.

"I thought I heard some familiar voices," she said comfortably. "You deserve to know what's going on. And I've told Mr. Canby as much. I don't think he particularly wants to see any of you right now, but that's just too bad, isn't it? Please, girls, come in."

They entered the foyer and all looked toward the fireplace, where Owen Canby stood with his back to them, his hands leaning on the marble mantle.

"Mr. Canby, I think you should tell the girls what you just told me. After all, they are as much involved as I at this point."

He turned to them, and for a moment, Dana's eyes locked with his. That hard glance wasn't nearly as intimidating, and she stared right at him, daring him to say anything awful to them.

"I don't really think this is something I wish to discuss with the students, Patrice," Owen Canby said gruffly.

"Don't you? Well, why not? They're going to know sooner or later, and I think it would be doing the decent thing to inform them yourself."

Her mention of "the decent thing" galvanized Mr. Canby into action. He started pacing the room, clearly troubled about the information he'd brought with him that morning.

"All right, yes, I agree, you do have a right to know. The Data-Tech deal fell through. There will be no sale of Canby Hall."

Dana kept staring at him. Faith and Shelley sat down hard on the nearest available piece of furniture, which was an armchair. Casey gave a war whoop, then immediately settled down. "You're kidding," she said.

"The adverse publicity was what finally changed their minds, apparently. But they also reassessed their financial status and discovered that the kind of building and reconstruction they'd have to do on this campus would have been prohibitive. They'd just received stats from their architects and technical people when the news stories broke. Consequently, they've forfeited their retainer, and they'll be looking elsewhere for a new property to buy."

He walked toward the girls, shaking his head slowly. "I haven't given up on the idea of selling this estate. I still feel that all my assets should be earning and growing steadily. But right now at least, I will be leaving things as they are. You can have your school . . . temporarily."

"But Mr. Canby," Shelley said shyly, with only a glimmer of a smile behind her blue eyes. "We *are* earning and growing. We have an endowment now. Didn't Ms. Allardyce tell you?"

He looked at the headmistress curiously, and she shrugged. "I didn't have time, Shelley."

"Somebody donated a great deal of money to the Save Canby Hall Committee this morning," Faith explained to him. "A great deal."

"We were going to use it to find a new property," Dana went on. "But now that we've got our old one back, we can start our endowment. And your board of trustees can invest it wisely and make us a . . . high-yield enterprise," she finished calmly. Then she walked directly toward him, her hand outstretched. "No hard feelings, Mr. Canby."

He looked at her for a moment with the kind of grudging admiration you have for a respected rival. Then he took her hand in a firm, strong grip and shook it. "You did it, girls," he said. "I never thought you would. Now tell me, what about this endowment? What was the amount of the check?"

"There wasn't any check," Ms. Allardyce cut in. "It was. . . ." She grinned at the girls again. "It was six shoeboxes full of money. In very large denominations. We have no idea who donated it."

Mr. Canby began to laugh. It started as a chortle, then progressed to a series of guffaws. When the tears were running down his cheeks, the girls joined in. It was hard to tell whether he was enjoying himself or was in terrible pain.

"Shoeboxes!" he finally gasped. "Oh, no! Oh, that old nut!" Then he wheeled to the door, plucked up his coat and hat, and started out toward his car. "You'll have this in writing today," he called back to Ms. Allardyce. The last thing they heard him say before he climbed into the Mercedes was, "Shoeboxes!"

"He's out of his mind," Casey nodded solemnly, watching him through the window.

"The man has snapped," Faith agreed. "See what money does to you?"

"But he knows who it is," Shelley said, snapping her fingers. "And I think I just might, too."

"Well, don't keep us in suspense," Dana demanded. "Who is it?"

"Call Chris," Shelley instructed her roommate. "And you call Johnny, Faith. I'm going to get hold of Tom. We're going to visit our benefactor."

Ms. Allardyce hadn't been able to get a word in. She was still trying to form a coherent sentence when the girls dashed past her out the door.

CHAPTER FOURTEEN

Tom had already left for school, his mother told Shelley over the phone, but Johnny, who was on a work-study program at Green-leaf High, promised he'd be right by with his pickup if his father would let him off from the gas station and garage, where he was now in charge of managing orders and doing accounts. Chris, who was in the midst of Study Week before exams, was only too happy to close his books and ride over to meet the girls.

"We're going to get so many demerits for cutting class, I don't even want to think about it," Faith sighed, as Johnny helped her up into the cab of the truck.

"How've you been, Faithie? I haven't seen you much lately," Johnny sighed, giving Faith a peck on the cheek. "Is that my fault or yours?"

"I think it's mine," she said softly. "I've been so involved with all the Save Canby Hall

problems, I haven't had a minute free. Sorry,"
she smiled up at him, letting him know how
much she'd missed him.

As Shelley and Casey clambered in beside
them, the two suddenly turned very business-
like. Neither one really felt comfortable about
showing what they felt for each other in
public. "Okay, where are we going? And
what's this all about, Shel?" Johnny demanded, his dark brown eyes amused but
skeptical.

"Shelley thinks she knows who just gave us
three million dollars," Casey explained with a
smirk. "So naturally, we're supposed to go on
a wild goose chase in and around Greenleaf to
find him and thank him."

"Just tell us who is it!" Dana stood beside
the truck waiting for Chris, and as she spotted
the Fiat Spider coming around the bend, she
waved him down. He pulled into the parking
lot just on the other side of the entrance to
the school.

"C'mon, we're all going with Johnny," she
explained, hauling him into the truck after
her.

"Dana, I heard something wonderful."
Chris began talking animatedly as Johnny
pulled out of the drive. "My father lost his
deal. He's not selling Canby Hall."

"Hey, that's old news," Casey shrugged.
"We've already seen your dad this morning.
Dana, tell him what he *hasn't* heard."

As Dana chattered happily about their

benefactor and the shoeboxes, Shelley directed Johnny down a side road that skirted the border of Greenleaf. They drove past open pasture land, and then through a dense, wooded section.

"Hey, who is this guy? Some kind of hermit?" Johnny grumbled as he put the truck in first gear to pull them up a steep hill.

"I've never actually been here, but Tom gave me a pretty good idea of where he lives. I'm sure this is the right road," Shelley said.

"Great, Pocahontas, and if it isn't?" Chris asked, tucking one arm comfortably around Dana's shoulders.

"Then we'll try the next road. This is important!" Shelley proclaimed. "Okay, Johnny, turn left over here, at that fork."

The truck carefully maneuvered the ruts and pockets of the old dirt road and started down a long, desolate stretch that led for several miles. There wasn't a house in sight.

"Aw, c'mon, Shel," Casey's voice cajoled her. "Give us a hint. Who's Santa Claus?"

"Uh-uh." Shelley looked like the cat who's eaten both the canary *and* the cream. "Wait till we get there."

"*If* we get there," Chris reminded her.

But just at that moment, a tiny puff of chimney smoke came into view on the horizon. Within seconds, they could see the little log cabin, standing all by itself in the distance. Behind it was a big red barn.

"That's it! We found it!" Shelley declared

triumphantly. "That's where he lives."

"Well, he can't complain about the over-crowded neighborhood," Casey shrugged.

As they approached the cabin, they could see a small figure bent over a wood stump. He was splitting logs for firewood with a rhythm and ease that belied his very evident age. Cary Sampton looked like he'd been chopping firewood all his life.

"Wait a second." Faith put one hand on Shelley's arm. "That's the guy who offered to bail us out of jail."

"That's right," Shelley smiled. "I guess you can park next to that old heap of his."

"But he could hardly come up with the hundred dollars," Dana reminded her. "He had to take it out of his shoe, for heaven's sake." Then she looked at the others curiously. "Shoe? Shoeboxes? You don't really believe. . . ."

"I certainly do," Shelley said. "Call it a hunch — call it what you like. I'm positive it's him. Hi, Mr. Sampton! How're you doing?" she called out the cab window. "Remember me?"

Cary Sampton stared at the truck as though it were a UFO that had just landed in his front yard. It was quite evident that he didn't get too many visitors.

"Well, yes, sure. You're Shelley, and those girls were with you at the jail. He was, too," he added, pointing at Chris. "Now how did you find me way out here?" he demanded, jabbing his ax back in the stump. He took off his hat, scratched his head, and sauntered over to the truck.

Shelley was already down on the ground and walking toward him. "I hope we're not intruding," she said politely. "But we really had to find you as soon as possible."

"Naw, it's okay. You, ah, you want to come in?" he asked hesitantly. "I can heat up some old coffee," he shrugged in his typical gruff way.

"That'd be great, sir," Chris smiled, taking Dana by the hand.

They followed Mr. Sampton inside the tiny cabin. The interior was simple, but nicely furnished with old oak pieces that looked positively burnished with age and care. The kids took seats on the braided rug that sat in the middle of the one room, and Mr. Sampton busied himself with heating the coffee on his woodstove and trying to find enough cups for everybody. As it turned out, Chris and Dana had to share one.

"Now, I've been a perfectly good host," Mr. Sampton nodded, drawing on the flannel shirt that he'd hung over one of his pressed-back kitchen chairs. "So you repay the favor. I think I have a right to know what you're doing here." He straddled the chair backwards and stared at them with his small, red-rimmed eyes.

"Well, Mr. Sampton," Shelley began. "Something pretty extraordinary happened at Canby Hall this morning. A messenger brought us six shoeboxes filled with money and an unsigned note. And on top of that, we can still have the Canby estate, because Owen Canby lost out on his deal with that computer company. This means the gift can go completely toward starting our endowment. So you see, we have to thank this person, whoever he is. You know everybody in town, and I figured you might just have a clue as to who's responsible for the gift. Do you?" She gazed at him innocently.

"I might," he said in his laconic style.

"It couldn't be you, could it?" Dana asked quietly.

"Might be." He shrugged. "Might not be. All depends." Mr. Sampton wasn't giving away a thing.

"Well. . . ." Casey just couldn't control herself. "Don't play hard to get. Tell us! If you like, it doesn't have to go any further than this room."

The old man looked at each one of them, peering into their very souls. Then he took a long draught of his coffee and put it down on the checkered tablecloth. "Aw, it's no good letting greenbacks lie around, anyhow. After all those years, they start going moldy."

Faith gasped; Casey choked on her coffee. Dana and Chris were beaming at the old man and Johnny still looked very confused. Only Shelley sat there smugly in the knowledge that she'd been right all along.

"But how . . . ?" Faith began. "I mean, it's just so *much!*"

"I tell you now, boys and girls, in the old days," Cary Sampton said, leaning back as though recounting a fable, "my family was kind of a big deal — sort of like the Canbys turned out to be later on. We Samptons had lots of land, and lots of dairy cattle, and then my crazy dad went out to Alaska for a spell and hit it rich on a gold mine."

"Really!" Johnny gave a disbelieving chuckle. "I thought all those gold-panners lost their shirts."

"Most did, son, most did. But my dad just kept looking till he found a rich vein. Then he tapped it and came home — didn't fiddle-faddle around. So once he came back to Green-leaf, he got himself a real smart Boston broker and he started investing in the stock market. This was, oh, I'd say, 1918, 1919, somewhere around there. By 1928, my dad had made his millions." He looked at the incredulous crew. "You wouldn't have known to look at him. He was just a simple man, a farmer for all intents and purposes. Nice guy."

"So what happened then?" Casey asked.

"Well, I don't know if a little bird told him or what, but round about the end of 1928, my dad pulled every cent he had out of the market. I mean *everything*. People, Horace Canby among them, told him he was out of his mind, but he didn't listen. He just took his gains and put 'em in shoeboxes. Didn't even trust the banks anymore. Got kinda strange and suspicious." He stood up and went to the front door. "C'mon, I'll show you where he hid the loot."

The group jostled their way out the door and followed Cary Sampton in back of the log cabin to the old red barn. It was pretty deserted except for two goats, who looked very disturbed when he turned on the overhead bulb, and some chickens squawking in their pens on the side of the barn. There were a lot of old tools and stalls where the cattle used to live, and even the stalls were still in good shape.

"Up here," he pointed over his head to the hayloft, "we kept the hay for the cows, see. We had thirty traps up there at one point. You could just open the traps, and the hay would fall down into each stall. Pretty handy." He prodded one with a pitchfork, and it opened, but nothing came out.

Then he walked across the floor to the grain bins and flipped one open. "I feed Grover Cleveland and Herbert Hoover out of this one." He nodded at the goats. "And the chicken feed's in this one." He showed them the next bin, which was filled with sacks of feed.

"One night, real late, my father wakes me and my brother up and tells us to come quiet-like. We tiptoe out to the barn, not waking my mom. My dad had about fifteen shoeboxes sitting there, all lined up.

" 'Whatcha gonna do with them, Dad?' asks my brother Walter, may he rest in peace. He died in '52.

"Dad says ,'Wall 'em in.' So he picked this here grain bin and hauled out the sacks. He got us some bricks and mortar and told us to get to work. We were both a lot thinner than him, see, so it was a little easier for us to bend over and get all the bricks nice and smooth. He said he wanted us to build a good, sturdy trough down here and wall in the shoeboxes.

" 'This money's your inheritance,' " he told us as we worked. " 'You ever need any of it when I'm alive, we'll discuss it. After my death, you split it equally with your ma. Do whatever you like with your share — I don't care. But for now, it stays put.' "

"This is absolutely incredible," Dana murmured.

"How much money do you think was in the boxes?" Chris asked.

"I don't think. I know. It was eight million, all together," Mr. Sampton told him. He threw back his head and laughed. "I must say, I thought my dad was a crackpot, but in those days, you didn't question your elders. We had enough to live on from the income of the farm and the lands, and we were comfortable. So we left the money right where it was." He patted the top of the bin.

"You mean it was all just sitting there since 1928?" Shelley demanded.

"Well, no. Now, you gotta understand what happened the next year," Mr. Sampton chuckled, folding his arms and looking at her.

"The stock market crashed," Chris said.

"And everybody lost everything. 'Cept my dad," Mr. Sampton said proudly. "He was cackling up a storm when it happened, screaming how he knew it, how he'd been smart. And he had, too."

"This is absolutely amazing," Casey muttered.

"So naturally, when Horace Canby came to him in 1930 and said it was time to get back in the market, now that the prices were low and all, they had this terrible fight. My dad told him to mind his business, and as far as I know, the two never spoke again in their lifetimes."

"But the money?" Johnny asked.

"Well, Walter took his share, and ma took hers when Dad died in '47, but then she passed on a year later, so Walter and I both had four million a piece. I left mine in the trough. Here's the last of it." He picked up three burlap sacks, displaying the destroyed brick trough underneath. Inside were two old shoeboxes. "You know where the other six are," he winked.

The girls were speechless. Then at last, Shelley came over and gave him a kiss on the cheek. Faith, Dana, and Casey all thanked him and embraced him. The poor old man was blushing so hard, you could see it even in the dim barn light.

"Now, don't carry on like that," he scoffed, pushing them away. "I would have made an endowment to your school long ago if I'd been able to forgive Horace Canby for that fight he had with my father. I guess I've been a stubborn old goat."

Chris, looking very pensive, walked over to shake Mr. Sampton's hand. "You put my family to shame, sir," he said fiercely. "I'd like to tell my father where the money's coming from."

Mr. Sampton reacted like he'd been scalded. "Don't you dare — you hear me? If you so much as breathe a word of what I've told you here, I'll deny it all."

"He knows, though," Shelley said softly. "When we mentioned that our donor had sent the funds in shoeboxes, he started laughing like he was going to burst. Then he said — oh, excuse me, Mr. Sampton, but I'm just quoting Owen Canby — he said, 'Why that old nut!' I guess your family secret's not so secret."

Mr. Sampton frowned and ran a hand over his face. "All right, then. Who knows, knows. But nobody else. Is that agreed?"

The six kids nodded at once, and only when Cary Sampton was satisfied that they were trustworthy did he let them out again into the light of day.

"So, I don't know about you," he said, just as if nothing at all had happened, "but I gotta get to work. Lots to do. I'll see you folks around. Can always find me at Pizza Pete's on senior citizen night, you know. They give discounts!" He gave them a big wink and, without further ado, walked back to his pile of logs. He was still splitting them when the kids drove off in the pickup several minutes later.

The ride back to campus was filled with laughter. Nobody was really in any mood to go back to class or study, and yet, they had no one to share their extraordinary news with, so they had to make do with acting silly while they were together. When Johnny dropped them at the front gates, promising to call Faith that evening, they were all in terrific moods.

"And what about us?" Chris asked when Dana walked him to his car.

"What about us?"

"I just wondered if you'd changed your mind about not seeing me anymore."

Dana smiled. "I'm seeing you now, aren't I?"

"So that means. . . . ?" He looked at her hopefully, his hazel eyes shining.

"I like you a lot, Chris. You're not the same guy I ran into running on the road that day, and yet you are. I'm not ready to go steady or anything like that, but I do want to get to know you better."

"I want that, too, Dana," he whispered. He took her head in his hands and drew his fingers softly down one cheek. She leaned toward him and felt the silvery glow of his kiss even before she felt his lips on hers. Then they hugged each other tightly, and Dana closed her eyes, enjoying the feeling of having him close to her.

When he sped down the road after promising to call, she turned back to the others, who had discreetly begun walking back toward the dorm. It was almost lunchtime, and they'd missed three classes, and they might be punished for it, but no one could have told from their faces that there was the least little thing wrong in the world.

"How did you know, Shelley?" Casey demanded, as they reached the door of Baker House. "He seemed like the last person in the world to have that kind of cash."

"Sometimes people who want to give you things kind of warn you about it first," Shelley said slowly.

"What do you mean?" Faith asked.

"I get it," said Dana, who had heard their last words as she caught up to them. "The bail money. It was more the way he was generous with us rather than the fact that he seemed to be hunting for every cent he gave. Is that it, Shel?"

"Yes, sort of. And then, too, it was just him. Tom said when we first met him that he was like a bowl of jelly inside all covered with sandpaper on the outside. It turned out to be a heart of pure gold instead of the jelly, but you get the point."

"I certainly do!" Faith grinned. Then she looked around, suddenly turning from the dorm doors to take in the whole view — the maple grove, the park, the wishing pool, the other buildings. "Look at this!" she exclaimed delightedly, throwing her arms out and spinning in a circle. "It's all ours."

"We get to stay here!" Casey shouted.

"We get to be together!" Shelley smiled.

"And we also get to be the very first generation of endowed Canby girls," Dana laughed happily.

They joined hands in a little circle on the brick path, oblivious to the glances of the girls who'd just been let out of their last morning classes. As the four of them drew together for a hug, the sun suddenly appeared from behind a cloud, welcoming them back to the estate that Horace Canby had declared theirs almost a century ago. Now, no matter what happened, they belonged to Canby Hall. No one could remove it from their hearts and minds, not ever.